P9-DBK-341

We Are the Scribes

ALSO BY RANDI PINK

Into White
Girls Like Us
Angel of Greenwood

We Are the Scribes

RANDI PINK

Feiwel and Friends
New York

A Feiwel and Friends Book
An imprint of Macmillan Publishing Group, LLC
120 Broadway, New York, NY 10271 • fiercereads.com

Copyright © 2022 by Randi Pink. All rights reserved.

Our books may be purchased in bulk for promotional, educational, or business use.
Please contact your local bookseller or the Macmillan Corporate and Premium Sales
Department at (800) 221-7945 ext. 5442 or by email at
MacmillanSpecialMarkets@macmillan.com.

Library of Congress Control Number: 2022907414

First edition, 2022
Book design by Michelle Gengaro-Kokmen
Feiwel and Friends logo designed by Filomena Tuosto
Printed in the United States of America

ISBN 978-1-250-82031-0 (hardcover)
1 3 5 7 9 10 8 6 4 2

"A dandelion crushed in a strong hand isn't destroyed, it is multiplied."

For Harriet Jacobs

My story ends with freedom.

Harriet Jacobs,
Incidents in the Life of a Slave Girl

Prologue

*The world burns and I sit quiet, incapable of anything.
It's a necessary burning. A scorching away of weaker forest to make
way for the newer, greener, fairer nation, if there is such a thing as
that. A nation where sixteen-year-old introverted Black girls like
me don't have to feel guilty for not knowing what to say or how to
say it. A nation where we don't fill up with pain and fear and anger
toward a system built for the sole purpose of keeping us quiet in the
first place. My hands feel too small to push against a mountain as
tall as racism. Today, like yesterday and the day before that, I am
a coward.*

"What you writing this time, Ruth?" asked my older sister,
Virginia. "Don't tell me it's that ridiculously sad, depression
shit again."

I didn't answer her, because she knew she was right.

"Where are you going?" I asked, watching as she tied her shoe in a triple knot so tight she'd have to use her teeth to get it out later. "It's not even eight in the morning."

Virginia crossed the bedroom in one energetic leap. "Revolution never sleeps, Baby Sister."

With surprising swiftness, Virginia snatched the pages from my grasp.

"Give it back!" I yelled. "That's private. Don't—"

But it was too late. She'd already read today's entry. With pity in her almond eyes, she handed it back and took a seat at the foot of her unmade twin bed. "Ruth."

"No," I replied. "Don't lecture me about how to feel."

"Ruth."

"No!" I repeated, staring at the floor to avoid her gaze.

"Ruth," she said, again crossing our small bedroom but this time slowly. "My quiet storm."

That's when I looked up. Virginia looked at me like I was made of something breakable. "You think I'm weak," I said.

"No," she said, kneeling in front of me, almost bowing. "I think you're valuable."

Virginia's slow, deliberate drawl drew out the most important words in her sentences. She threw away the first three in a jumble and hung on to the last like it was the only one that mattered—*valuable*. Such a phenomenal word, *valuable*.

There was a knock on the bedroom door—our dad. "We've got to go," he said to Virginia. "Protest's about to start."

"We'll talk later on." She bounded toward the door.

"Wait," I said, desperate to know what she'd meant. "Valuable how?"

Virginia cracked the door and told Dad, "Just a second, okay?"

"Seriously, Virginia." His voice deepened. "I will not miss this one. Mayor's taking down the monument."

But Virginia had already come back to sit next to me on my bed. Her dainty hand gently swept my cheek, the metal from rings on all five of her fingers cool against my skin.

"You're a scribe of the movement. An illuminator. Our Harriet Jacobs. I'm a dime a dozen. A trend on TikTok. But you, my love, are a writer."

"You're so much more than a trend on—"

"I'm out." Dad's voice vibrated from frustration. "Meet me at the Linn statue."

Virginia rolled her eyes and smiled. "He always threatens to leave me and never does." She grabbed hold of my cheeks and pressed her forehead to mine.

"Promise me, Ruth. My sweet, wise, quiet storm. No matter what happens. Promise me you'll write this moment."

Self-conscious about morning breath, I attempted to pull away, but she wouldn't allow it. "I stink," I told her.

"I don't care," she replied, almost angrily. "Promise me. Do it right now."

"Of course I'll write," I said, trying not to blow bad breath into her beautiful face. "I can't help but to—"

"No," she interrupted sternly. "Promise you'll write it honest. Even the horrible parts. Just like Harriet did. Promise me."

"I promise."

And she let me go.

We heard the garage door lift and close. "He actually left me this time," she said, springing to her feet. "Guess I'll have to walk. Bye, Love."

"Wait," I said. "Who's Harriet?"

She winked in response.

That's the last time I ever saw my stunning live wire of a big sister.

1

"Ready for this?" Dad asked across our thick wooden dining table. "You don't have to go to school."

I couldn't think of anything to say in response. Instead, I stared at the extra-large stockpot of cheese and veggie eggs. He'd perfected them, because that was his way of dealing with things.

I checked his clean-shaven face. He'd perfected that, too. In the days after Virginia, constant YouTube videos blasted from his bathroom on how to get rid of his beard. He'd grown it long and scraggly before and I'd liked it. Coupled with his red-rimmed glasses and neat sweater vest, he looked like the African American history professor that he was. Ever since that horrible day, he'd gotten rid of the scraggle and hung the sweater in the back of the closet, exchanging it for pressed suits.

Now, he looked like a banker.

"You don't have to speak if you don't want to," he said before getting back up to stir the eggs. "They're getting clumpy just sitting here."

For the sixth time since we'd sat down, he began whipping the nonexistent lumps away.

"More OJ?"

He bounced up. I shook my head and kept quiet. I'd begun counting my daily words again. It wasn't quite seven in the morning and I'd said none so far. I don't know why I was doing it. Maybe I was saving them for a larger moment to release all at once.

Dad sat back down for exactly four seconds, hummed a tune, and jumped back up. Polar opposite of me, he hated stillness and silence with a passion.

"Do you hear the baby crying?" he asked, chugging extra-hot coffee without flinching. "I think I do."

He took off, leaving me alone with the eggs and the OJ that I didn't ask for.

Virginia had been his favorite, but I couldn't blame him. Virginia was everyone's favorite. She knew what to say. Always. She didn't overthink it. Empathy flowed directly from her heart and through her lips without taking any stops on the way. Virginia and Dad especially, their souls matched. Orange and blue. Yellow and purple. Red and green. Complementary. He and I, on the other hand, well, we were different.

He sprang back into the room holding Melody, my one-year-old sister. She was more like me than anyone in the world. Another quiet storm on the horizon. I smiled at her and she smiled back.

"Ruuuuu!" She reached and leaned for me and I took her.

I wanted to tell her good job for getting my name right on the first try, but I didn't want to waste words. Melody had started accidentally calling me other names. She'd stutter through Virginia and Ruuu and Mama and Dada until she'd finally give up and go quiet like me. Melody's smile never lasted all that long anymore, either. That morning, she sat in my lap, calmly and deliberately picking apart my plate of eggs with her fingers and frowning.

She missed our mom.

"Your mother should be home next weekend," Dad said, sensing it, too. "Senate recess is coming up soon. Hopefully."

He added *hopefully* to the end because the last three recesses had been canceled. The nation was coming apart, so my mother had stationed herself in Washington, DC, to help put it back together. I saw her face every night on the news. She rotated now from MSNBC to CNN and sometimes even FOX. I was proud that my mom had steel balls enough to raise her voice on the network's highest-rated evening show, *Todd and Tracy Talk About the Day*. She was a badass. Dad was a badass. And somehow they had a coward like me.

"Sure you're ready for this?" Dad asked again. "Everyone will . . . The school knows that . . . It might be . . ."

I nodded and got up from my chair.

"You'll drop off Melody, then?" he asked with both sympathy and pleading in his eyes.

He looked so much like Virginia when he did that. They shared the crooked worry-wrinkle just above their left brow and a frown dimple on the right cheek. His was visible again, now that he looked like a banker with no beard. It was both beautiful and heartbreaking.

I hoisted Melody into a wrapped scarf I used as a sling and made my way downstairs. Melody's day care was a block away from my school, and both were walking distance from our apartment building. Before leaving, Melody forced her head back to lock concerned eyes with me.

"Virgin . . . Mama . . . Dada . . ." Melody sputtered her way toward my name. She gave up just before she reached it and hung her head on my chest in frustration.

Ten years ago, my parents moved us into downtown Birmingham. It'd been a ghost town back then—all empty buildings and blight. Everyone told them it was a horrible idea to buy a whole building downtown. I remember sitting around the Thanksgiving table, listening to aunts and uncles and friends say they were making a mistake. But my parents were stubborn, as most brilliant people are.

With two small children in tow, they sold the cookie-cutter cul-de-sac monstrosity and bought the brick shell of what used to be a radio repair shop with two apartments above it. Virginia and I thought it was an adventure. Running loops around the dusty concrete. Up and down rickety staircases that were probably not safe. We loved it and so did our parents.

Most parents might have fought constantly in such chaos, but mine were never more in love than they were back then. Building something together—a family, a home, a life unique. We all were. Now, ten years later, Melody and I walked the street that used to be empty buildings and homeless tents, past quaint coffee shops, lofts, and law firms. Gentrified. Our building alone was now worth at least a couple million dollars. But our happy family broke. Mom ran away to Washington. Dad looked like a banker. And Virginia, well, Virginia . . .

As I walked the newly power-washed sidewalks, it occurred to me just how long it'd been since I'd left my building. Time got away from me sometimes, especially now.

Approaching Melody's day care, I spotted a nearly faded BLACK LIVES MATTER sign crooked in the front window. When I opened the door, everyone inside stopped and stared at us. No one knew what to say, and none of them wanted to be the first to say the wrong thing. Silent gloom came over the place.

Feeling pressure to help them feel comfortable, I spoke my first word in days. "Hi," I said, and they all said it back.

Melody remained silent, and I wondered if it was a good

idea to leave her there. This was a fishbowl and she was the fish to be gawked at. But I had no choice; I couldn't take her to school with me. I signed my name and tucked her in at a table of staring one-year-olds. It seemed that even they knew she was the sister of the girl who had died.

It took me less than six minutes to reach the front doors of my high school. I'd never been noticed there before and had no desire to be seen. Actually, I rather enjoyed making my way through hallways unacknowledged. Or if I was, only as the kid sister of beautiful, charismatic Virginia.

They all knew me now.

Snaking through the halls, every one of them looked and weren't nearly as cautious as the day care staff.

"There she is!"

"Ruth! Ruth! Saw your mom on the news! Your dad, too!"

"That's her! That the sister!"

The sister, someone had said. That's the sister.

Insensitive fucking morons. I didn't even make it to first period. Eight minutes later, I was back at Melody's day care to sign her out. She dug her nails into my arm the entire walk home and squealed with joy when I opened the front door.

She waddled to her room, surely to find her beloved Qai Qai doll, and I noticed a single letter had been dropped through the mail slot. Well, not a letter in the traditional sense. It looked more like an old-timey scroll with a black wax closure marked with an *H*. I picked it up to find my name handwritten on the side of the beige parchment. And underneath my name, the golden seal with a loopy *S* in the center surrounded by the blocky-type words—WE ARE THE SCRIBES.

I opened it.

2

"I was born a slave."

That was the first line of my book, you see? They call it <u>Incidents in the Life of a Slave Girl</u>.

I'm Harriet. And like you, I write to keep from screaming out. You have a fancy thing to write with. Just a tap of the fingertips and words appear perfectly, beautifully before you. I would have loved such an instrument. Surely, that would have benefited me greatly in the attic. But we'll get to that later.

I truly was born a slave. A fortunate one, however, if you can believe that there is such a thing. I imagine you can't grasp the concept, but it surely existed for a short time.

When my parents lived, I had no idea I was enslaved. They sheltered us, you see? My brother, John, and I. With kisses and warmth and even sweets. Where'd we acquire sweets? Ah, my grandmother's mistress allowed her to bake if she finished all of her chores. And John and I got the broken crackers, and too-brown crusts. Our bellies never roared and our faces never dried from the kisses of our mother. But, oh dear girl, when slavery hit, it hit hard.

I write you this because that is what we do—we write. We are the Scribes, you see? And alone, terrified, and trapped in the attic we'll talk about later, a Forescribe sent me letters just as I'm sending letters to you now. Those letters kept me breathing in the tightest of spaces, and more importantly than breathing, those letters kept me writing.

Even way back in 1861, the book I wrote altered the world as I knew it. You too have a work within you that will change everything for you. This, I know, must feel like an insurmountable charge. And you will want to quit every day.

Don't.

You must write. It is what you were placed on this earth to do.

Your Forescribe,
Harriet

3

"Harriet Jacobs," I inadvertently said out loud, studying the loopy handwriting.

I ran my index finger along the perfect circles and coils and twists of the writing. Actually, it was more calligraphy. Unrealistic in its precision. The type of writing that takes too long to bother with these days. A writing from a different time.

Then, I thought, *1861. I was born a slave. Incidents in the life of a* . . . Untouchable memories nearly knocked me down. I grabbed ahold of the kitchen island and squeezed for stability. I forced my eyes shut and heard my father's voice in my mind, but it was his voice before Virginia had been snatched away from us. Filled with optimism and hope for tangible change. I heard Virginia, too. Young and twirling Virginia—eight or nine years old.

I heard him read, "'I was born a slave.'" And then his voice became more and more distant, like I was falling asleep as he spoke.

Then, for the first time since she left me, I heard Virginia. She said, "You are the scribe of these times. An illuminator. Our Harriet . . ."

I leaped when Melody tugged on my pant leg and signed for *hungry*. With the recent stuttering, she'd been reverting back to the few signs I'd taught her when she was smaller.

I wanted to reread this strange scroll another four times. I longed to investigate how it arrived and where it could have come from. What strange trick was someone playing? What cruel joke?

But when Melody was hungry, I had to jump to it. Not because she was a demanding child. The opposite, actually; she rarely ate at all so when she wanted to, I took immediate heed, abandoning the scroll.

I reached into the freezer and pulled out an unopened FedEx box of breast milk that Mom had pumped and shipped from DC, thawed a pouch, and mixed it with squash and peas picked from Dad's rooftop garden. Melody had only eaten food either grown with our hands or extracted from our mother's body. Of that, I was proud. After a quick temperature check, Melody bounded off, balancing her bowl with such concentration. I watched her until she settled in the recliner.

Then I read the letter again. And I reread it before rolling it back into a tight cylinder. I placed the letter on my clean dining room table and watched it, waiting for it to do something. When it didn't, I picked it up again and reread it.

I opened my laptop and searched the words *Harriet* and *attic*.

The first page was dominated by two bald eagles mating on something called an attic branch. I kept searching and only found more bald eagles, attic insulation, and information on how to remove branches from one's attic. I closed my laptop before swirling too far down that rabbit hole.

I longed for Virginia. She would know without having to look it up. She would speak without worrying if she was wrong because she'd be right. About everything. And then I remembered. She'd called me Harriet Jacobs once. Months ago, before she . . . left.

After a quick look at Melody, I headed to the upstairs library. In the early years, it was my favorite place in our apartment. Dark green shelving covered every wall, and every space was filled with books.

Back then, my mother obsessed over transforming the space into a hobbit hole. Pinpoint twinkle lights, plush plaid overstuffed armchairs, and squatty lamps with sheer fabric draped over them. She succeeded so epically that

Architectural Digest requested a four-page spread featuring our third floor.

I hated going in there lately, though. It was marvelous, there was no denying that, but Virginia was still in there. So much so, I could hardly concentrate on the beauty of the space. All I saw was Virginia everywhere I looked.

She was in the antique wooden desk that had been locked for years, and no one knew where the key was. Virginia believed the key would turn up. No way they'd just throw such a thing away, she'd tell me. It's in a drawer somewhere or a jewelry box or one of those Christmas cookie tins, I swear it is, Sis, you'll see.

She was in the mindfulness mats she'd stacked in the far corner for anyone who needed a moment to meditate. Time out is a good idea, she'd once told me. Not just for children, for all of us. Human beings desire time to think, and in this world, that can feel out of reach. And now, the mats were collecting dust.

She was in the four copies of *The Autobiography of Malcolm X*, one for each of us; she'd placed them around the Christmas tree two years prior. One for Mom since she's "a fighter rare." One for Dad because he "won't shut up about the man." One for herself because "I know he's dead and all but I will marry a man that fine, you mark my words." The last one for me since "Malcolm X wasn't born Malcolm X. He was born Little, like you, and, You, my quiet storm, will roar one day. I can feel it."

I could go on and on finding bits of Virginia up there. So many that I might be able to build a whole person right in the third-floor library. But I didn't dare risk it. I would have to be in and out before I broke down.

I stormed inside the open room with my index finger ready to scan the titles, organized alphabetically by author. As I scanned, I mouthed the letter *J*, but didn't say it aloud as not to waste words. In that moment, it occurred to me that I wasn't even wasting words when I was the only one around to hear them. It had never gotten that bad before. I reached *J*. Harriet Jacobs's book should've been right there. It wasn't.

Beneath me, I heard the muffled cries of my little sister. She must've just noticed I'd left. I lowered my finger and went to Melody.

Later than evening, my dad opened the door holding twelve glazed donuts from Cahaba Fields Sweet Shop downstairs. Melody, oblivious to what a donut was, didn't flinch at the sight of them. Instead, she kept pretend-reading her picture book. I, however, was completely shocked at the sight of them.

I'd never seen my dad eat anything he hadn't grown on the roof or ordered from the farm. Eggs, milk, cheese, butter were delivered weekly, and even quarter cows came from a farmer we visited every six months. Dad didn't believe in anything fake. Fake people, fake friends, fake history. And there he was, holding on to quite possibly the fakest food on earth, donuts.

"Hi," he said through tired eyes. And that's when I noticed the expression on his face. He hurt. Bad.

He whisked Melody high into the air. "You checked out of school?"

I nodded.

"And you got her out, too?"

I nodded.

"You don't have to go back," he said to the donuts. "Ever, if you don't want to. You can finish this year virtual if you want. You're way ahead in your school work anyway."

Something was happening inside him. Something similar, I thought, to what was happening in me. His something manifested itself on the outside. My something seethed inside like a working spore.

"Ah, there's your mother," he said with a new depth of disdain in his voice.

I glanced at the muted television to see her beautiful brown face not smiling. I smiled at her not-smiling face, because only the strongest among us don't smile when they know millions of people are watching. The easiest way to gain favor with an audience is to cheese like an idiot. My mother didn't. She, instead, stared straight at the camera speaking the truth. Melody saw her, too, and somehow figured out how to unmute the television.

"No, Lillian, thank you for having me," she said to the

short-haired host who had recently left NPR for MSNBC. "It's an honor to be on your show."

"The honor, Senator, is mine," the host said in response. "I'd like to get right to it, if you don't mind. But please allow me to express my utmost condolences for the loss of your daughter. The strength to keep going, well, that must be the most inspiring thing I've ever seen."

"Pshhhha!" My dad let out an almost guttural disapproval.

I stared at him for a moment, but he didn't notice. He was watching his wife, the woman he'd worshipped, with the kind of look he reserved for Republicans.

"Inspiring," Mom said. "I don't know about that—"

"No, ma'am," Lillian interrupted. "I have to stop you there. As soon as you heard about your beloved daughter's death, you flew home straightaway. And the day after the funeral, you flew right back to DC to introduce legislation that will officially label the Ku Klux Klan as a terrorist group. Is that correct?"

"Actually . . ." My mother paused but didn't smile. "I flew back immediately after the funeral. Didn't even make the lowering of the casket."

"Well," my dad yelled at the television. "The rest of us were there, Velicia."

I shot him a look that I was certain he'd notice, but he didn't. He just kept steaming, all of his attention on the television.

"That's the most incredible thing I think I've ever heard."

"Thank you, Lillian," my mother said. "But I really must make this short. I have to pump so I can ship this breast milk to my one-year-old."

"Okay, yes, yes, yes." Lillian began rustling papers and fumbling. She clearly was not expecting that.

"Sly minx," Dad said under his breath. "Your mother's becoming a damn good politician, I must say."

"May I take the lead for a moment?" My mother asked and didn't wait for a response. "I bring that up intentionally, Lillian. I am a US senator. Citizen elected to the first branch of coequal government, yet I must wait twelve painful hours until I have an opportunity to adequately pump my breasts to nourish my child. And even you, as accomplished as you are, seem uncomfortable with the subject."

"I," Lillian started. "I just wasn't expecting—"

"I meant zero offense, Lillian. For this reason, tomorrow morning I will introduce legislation to incorporate a mandatory hour of breastfeeding into every workday for lactating mothers."

Lillian pressed her earpiece as if getting word from her producers. "Okay, okay, really? Yes."

"Are you listening to me, Lillian?"

"Yes, ma'am, but—"

"All women deserve the right to feed their children," my mom continued. "I understand that this topic is not popular, but it must be addressed immediately. Just yesterday, I spoke with a constituent who was forced to pump milk in her car. Unacceptable!"

"Ma'am?"

"No," my mom said, dominating this poor woman's show like it was her own. I felt both proud and embarrassed. "Lactation is painful enough without holding milk in for some CEO to figure out it's an important enough issue to pay attention to."

"Ma'am?"

"No woman should have to pump in her car—"

"Madam Senator, are you the vice presidential nominee?" Lillian asked this so quickly that I had to run the words back through my mind a few times to understand them. "My producers have just gotten word that CNN broke the news moments ago. Is that why you're appearing on my show tonight? To announce that you've accepted the position of vice presidential nominee on the Democratic ticket?"

My mother smiled for the first time since she'd been on camera. She didn't just smile, she plastered on the fakest grin, like a contestant in the Miss America pageant.

"Ma'am?" Lillian asked calmly. "Should congratulations be in order?"

"I-I," my mother stuttered through bared teeth. "I haven't shared this news with my family yet, but—"

"Ah!" Lillian interrupted. "Congratulations, then, ma'am! I must admit here in front of my audience and you and everyone that I was secretly hoping Harrison would choose you as his running mate. You have everything this country needs and more. And Senator, good luck with your breast-feeding initiative. Would you hold tight while we take a quick break?"

My mother nodded and smiled until her beautiful smiling face was replaced by a commercial about paper towels.

"What the actual fuck?" my dad yelled out and then disappeared into his bedroom.

4

I let the box of donuts sit unopened on the counter until my dad came back into the kitchen, cell phone in hand, for the second segment. He fumed, arms folded, staring at the television. When Mom came back on the screen, he threw the phone on the counter and it slid in front of me so I could easily read the all-caps text he'd sent to her during the commercial break.

YOU DARE ACCEPT THIS SHIT WITHOUT
TELLING ME!! YOU HAVE CHILDREN! DO YOU
REMEMBER THAT? A ONE-YEAR-OLD BABY GIRL!
A GRIEVING SIXTEEN-YEAR-OLD WHO'S GONE
FUCKING MUTE! YET YOU STILL GALAVANT
AROUND, TALK SHOW TO TALK SHOW, WITH

ZERO REGARD FOR THE ONLY PEOPLE IN THE
WORLD WHO ACTUALLY GIVE A SHIT ABOUT
YOU! I NEVER AGREED TO BE YOUR MISTER
MOM! I SHOULDNT HAVE TO WORK AND COOK
AND CLEAN AND TEACH AND COMFORT AND
CARE FOR TWO CHILDREN ALL BY MYSELF!
THIS IS NOT EVEN POSSIBLE! YOU DARE!!!!!

Her response: Women do it every day. Grow up.

As soon as I finished reading the text exchange, Mom reappeared on the television, no longer smiling.

"Welcome back to *Lillian Tonight*," the host announced. "In case you missed our breaking news, Velicia Fitz is the official vice presidential nominee for the Democratic Party. And if you catch me squealing, you will know that I was hoping for this. Congratulations again, ma'am."

"Thank you, Lillian," Mom said, poker face back on. "It is an honor to stand alongside Mr. Jim Harrison, the future president of the United States. This will be a long journey toward November. And an astronomical undertaking not only for me, but also for my exceptional husband, Jo, who has been working while caring for our children for over six months now. And Lillian, he's done it without complaint. Only support. Every working woman should have such a support system."

"Ah, yes," Lillian beamed. "If you're watching, Mr. Fitz, you're a saint."

They chuckled together. "He is that." My mother winked at the camera.

I looked at my father, who, for the first time since he'd walked in the door, looked slightly amused. She'd softened him somehow, right there through the television. Good one, Mom. She was becoming a helluva politician.

"But this will be taxing on your children as well, I presume."

"They are very strong," Mom answered. "We'll get through this together."

"Madam Vice Presidential Nominee," Lillian smiled. "That's all the time we have on *Lillian Tonight*. Thank you, Senator, for being with us tonight. And best of luck on tomorrow's legislation."

"Thank you, Lillian."

"Signing off. Until tomorrow, that's all for *Lillian Tonight*."

Dad's phone buzzed and he dove for the counter to catch the call.

"Yes, hello," he answered. "Okay." He hung up. "She wants to do a video call with all of us."

A moment later, Melody's iPad lit up.

"Hey, y'all," Mom said, sounding so much more like my mother than she had on television. She allowed her southern to show with us in ways she didn't in public. "Sorry 'bout that. Give me a minute to hook up this pump before we get into it. I'm in pain over here."

"Maaaaamaaaa!" said Melody. "Mama! Mama! Mama!"

I wanted to tell Melody "good job."

"One minute, Mama's baby girl. Let me just press go on this . . ."

Mom's eyes rolled back into her head as the milk began to flow into the clear bags. FedEx boxes arrived on our doorstep every other day filled with them, and the freezer was beginning to overflow.

"Thank God," she said. "That feels better."

"Mama! Mama! Mama!"

"What the hell do you think you're doing?" Dad interjected, startling Melody and making Mom scowl.

I was wondering the exact same thing. What the hell was she doing? Signing us up to trek up and down the country without as much as a courtesy call to let us know first. I was too overwhelmed to make it to first period, after all. And that was before I even knew my mother was running for vice president of the United States. The whole country would rip us to shreds.

"I'm jumping on an opportunity that anyone would in my situation," she replied, putting her TV personality voice back on. "Do you have any idea how many of my colleagues would kill for this opportunity?"

"I don't give a damn about your colleagues!" Dad yelled at Melody's iPad. "This is about us!"

"I understand that, Joseph," she said in her politician's tone, which at this moment made me want to yell at the iPad right along with my dad.

"Oh, I'm Joseph now, huh?" he said. "Read your texts, Velicia. We're falling apart down here."

"I read the texts," she said, seemingly unaffected. "All caps? Come on, man."

"Mama! Mama! Mama!"

I grabbed my dad's arms to pull him away from the iPad. Melody was desperate to speak to our mother, and our father wasn't noticing.

"Mama! Mama! Mama!"

Melody smashed her face into the camera, and that's when my real mother showed up.

"How you doin', Mama's baby girl?" she asked with tears in her eyes and a deep furrow in her brow. "I miss you, too, beautiful baby. You're so big! Stop getting so big! Oh my sweetheart. Can I tell you something?" My mother whispered into the camera. "When you were in Mama's belly, you spoke with the clearest of voices. Like Maya Angelou or Malcolm X. You will speak life to the masses. I just know that you will. You'll stand in front of the multitude. You, Mama's baby girl, bring with you change. I just know it."

"Velicia?"

"Yes, Joseph?"

"Have you really accepted this nomination?"

She sat up straight. "I most certainly have."

My father swiped her face away, ending the video call before I had a chance to be noticed by my mother.

5

That night, I dreamed that I was speaking again. I spoke with such confidence that, as soon as I opened my mouth, I knew it was a dream. There was no way I'd speak like that in real life. I stood in front of thousands, maybe hundreds of thousands, of cheering people. They were waiting for someone. I'd assumed they were waiting for my mom and I was the opening act.

But there I was. Standing tall, without the crippling nerves that usually halted my words on their way from my heart to my lips.

"Welcome, ladies and gentlemen!"

I had to pause for thunderous applause. I stepped back from the microphone as if to welcome it. I felt myself naturally accepting ovation. Almost reveling in it.

In the crowd, I honed in on a small child atop her mother's shoulders. The girl had two afro puffs on the very top of her head and the back was flying loose, not quite long enough to reach the puffs. As I drank in praise, I read her shirt. It said WE ARE THE SCRIBES in golden and black loopy, sparkly letters.

I stepped back to the microphone. "Listen!"

That single word brought the large crowd to a quick halt.

"Speak, Sis!" said a voice from the crowd. "Speak!"

"Every family represented within the sound of my voice, hear me," I said to them. "Hear. Me! I feel you all searching for a leader among us. You may think you've found this leader in me."

"Wooooo!!!!"

"Thank you," I said to the elderly woman who'd let out that encouragement. "I am not ready to lead, ma'am."

"You are a queen!"

"Thank you," I said to the young boy in the third row. "But I see so many pressured into speaking before they're ready. I see them canceling themselves like chess pieces on a board. I see potential trailblazers gobbled up by minor mistakes. I am not your hero. Not today."

"Well," asked the girl with the afro puffs. "If it's not you, who is it?"

I felt a firm tap on my shoulder and the crowd cheered even louder. As I slowly turned to see who was behind me, I woke up without getting a glimpse.

I sat up in bed attempting to count the words I'd spoken within my dream as if they counted. But there was no use, the dream was slipping from my memory, as dreams do. I got up and stood beside my bed, trying to mimic the posture I'd had within my dream while I could still remember.

"Ginia . . . Maaaamaaa . . . Daaaaaadaaaa. . . . Ruuuuuuu!" Melody stuttered in the moonlight.

The creaking floor must've woken her up. She'd been making her way to my bedroom for weeks now. So quietly that I didn't even know she was there. She'd curl up into a tight ball and fall asleep on the plush rug next to my bed. I kept telling her she could climb in, but she preferred the floor to her crib and my bed and anywhere else.

By the time I lifted her into a tight hug, memory of my dream was almost gone.

"Ruuu!" she said, finally getting it on the first try and seeming extremely proud of that fact. "Ruuuuuuuuuu!"

"Good job, Baby Girl," I told her with four words spoken out loud. "No, that was an outstanding job," I said, using six more.

6

I rocked Melody back to sleep and placed her on the rug. That's when I noticed a text message from my mother. A longing shot through my body. It was unconscious and uncontrollable, and I had no idea I'd wanted so badly for her to notice me.

> Ruth. Your father told me you aren't speaking.
> Why?

That was the message in its entirety. That's it? Nine words. Were nine words enough to send to the daughter who'd gone selectively mute? I closed my phone, deciding not to answer her.

I knew she was busy. Too busy to compose a proper text.

Penning legislation for lactating moms, accepting calls from potential presidents of the United States, holding conference calls with the most important people on this earth, but me? I got nine words.

She definitely didn't deserve a reply.

Instead, I lifted the scroll and reread it in the moonlight. WE ARE THE SCRIBES, it said. The same phrase on the T-shirt of the little girl in my dream.

Whoever had sent it had it wrong. Because I was no longer writing. I couldn't. Since Virginia, I hadn't been able to sit in a quiet place for long enough to do it. I'd only write about her and it would break me. A writer is a dangerous thing to be, after all. To scribe is to open oneself up to more criticism than anybody should accept.

I placed the scroll back onto my nightstand and listened to the sweet sound of my little sister snoring in the night. I fell asleep and into a place where there was no dream.

7

When I woke up, Melody was gone and I knew I'd
overslept. I glanced at the clock on my bedside table—10:37
a.m. I leaped up. I hadn't slept that long in months. Melody
would surely be wet and my dad would've left for work.
I rushed into the front room without taking the time to
brush my teeth.

"Hey, Sleepyhead," said Dad.

I nearly fell over with surprise to see him bouncing
Melody on the living room floor. He'd skipped his 9:30
class. I'd never known him to skip out on any of his classes,
ever. Even when he'd been offered a yearlong paid sab-
batical, still, he volunteered to teach. And when Virginia . . .
He went back that next Monday morning. He loved it too
much to skip it, or so I thought.

"Another conference call," he said solemnly. "This time with all of them."

All of who? Who was there other than Mom, I wondered. When my dad swiped the iPad, I got my answer.

"Hi, Fitzes!" announced Jim Harrison, the presidential nominee of the Democratic Party. "You must be Melody!"

Melody squinted at the iPad. Did she recognize him from the news?

"And you." He spoke to me like I was someone to impress. "You, young lady, must be Ruth. I have a sister named Ruth, do ya' know? My favorite, too. But don't you dare tell the rest of 'em or I'll deny it." He spoke in a forced North Dakota hokeyness and smiled enough to show his too-white veneers.

I nodded.

"A woman of few words," he said, smiling. "Rare. She should coach my wife."

I couldn't force myself to laugh at that because it wasn't funny. Not only the crack about me, but also the fact that he didn't have the decency to call the woman he was married to by her name. *My wife* was not a name, after all. In response to my silence, he cleared his throat.

"I'd like to introduce you to my daughter," he continued. "She's exactly your age. Isn't that a hoot? Judy!" he yelled outside view of the camera.

"Whaaat?" I heard her singsong reply in the distance.

I'd seen her standing beside him when he'd won the

nomination. If she actually was my age, she was small and she looked like a nervous wreck with ants in her pants. I knew her name was Judy because after that appearance at her father's side, she'd gone viral. They nicknamed her Loony Judy with #loonyjudy being the top worldwide trending hashtag on Twitter that evening.

She appeared on the screen beside her father with her hair wild and out of place. Her enormous glasses held on for dear life at the tip of her nose. And she smiled crooked and twitchy like her cheek was being pulled by an invisible bit of string.

"Ruth Fitz!" She announced my name like she was introducing me at an assembly. "Why, I've heard all about you."

I wanted to laugh. Not *at* her like everyone else, but still, I wanted to laugh.

"I feel that we'll get along famously!" She bowed and stared at the camera, waiting for me to reply.

"Me too," I said out loud, and everyone's head shot around, even Melody's.

"Ruuu!"

"Looking forward!" she said. "I have to get back. Theatre camp starts tomorrow and I'm learning lines from *Little Shop of Horrors*. I'm shooting high this year and auditioning for the part of Audrey. You know the work?"

I shook my head.

"Oh no," she said. "Well, we'll have to fix that! See ya'."

She exited left.

"That's our Judy," said Mr. Harrison. "Named after Judy Garland, wouldn't ya' know? Poor dear still thinks she's doing that ridiculous musical when Secret Service will barely even allow us out of our hotel rooms."

Mr. Harrison wreaked of something I did not like.

"Where is Velicia, Jim?" Dad asked. I could tell that he was trying to show respect, but the question came out wrong and nearly impolite.

"Oh," Mr. Harrison said, smiling and attempting charm. "She was tied up in committee, whatever that means."

I hoped he knew what it meant. Seriously.

"When will she be on the call?"

"Again, Mr. Fitz," he said, now meeting my father's stiff tone. "She is held up."

"Okay, then, Mr. Presidential Nominee," Dad said, outright rude. "I have to get back to work."

He hung up without saying goodbye and I knew, then and there, these two men fighting over my mother would not end well.

Dad left in a huff. As he did, he stepped right over a second scroll without noticing it.

I watched it sit there for a short while, nervous to approach. I'd explained the first scroll away in my mind as someone trying to mess with us. Especially after my mother's announcement, it all made sense. An unwelcome quirk of major politics was random people trying to throw off my family, which is why I rejected social media of any kind. But there was another one. This meant there were now two options: Either I had a stalker or I was losing my grip on reality.

I went to it.

8

Dear, Scribe—

You are in a crisis of silence. I've been there before, and for the likes of us, this is a dangerous place. No one understands the quiet mind of a Scribe. It can be simultaneously treacherous and calm, like a recluse brown spider. You must find your way out soon or you will have to stay there.

I regret implying about the attic without telling the entirety of that story. Such things nag Scribes like us—don't they?

My intention is not to evade, but you will not understand fully the attic without backstory. Also, I regret to ask: Please do not read my book yet. You will not understand this until you've released one of your own, but it is rude to read a Scribe's work. Counterintuitive? Yes. And still, quite true. I have a brief anecdote.

After my book's publication, I spent several nervous months hoping I wouldn't run into anyone who'd actually read the thing. I'd avoided them, mostly by holing up in my home, until the festivities of Christmas were upon me, and well-meaning friends and family members surrounded my person. They bombarded me with questions about whether my book was selling, and why I'd chosen to include specific antics, and the attic, oh dear! Everyone asked how oh how I could sustain my sanity under such circumstances.

The moral: Don't read my book until after we've finished our interactions.

Alas, I digress.

I know you hurt. But I regret to inform you that pain is a part of being an artist. It is also a part of being a woman. And a Black one, well, no one said it would be easy, did they? My advice in this moment, for what it is worth, is do not allow your mind to dominate your being. We are charged with keeping track of whole lives within our singular minds. Worlds are built between our ears and this can drive a girl wild. Too, the internal is undervalued by most, but for you and me, it's where life exists. Still, you will need someone you can lay your head upon.

For me, it was my children. While I could not touch them then, I watched. Every day, I watched them grow and explore and grin in the midst. For you, my dear girl, there must be one respectable person in your life. Find them soon, or you will stay in your funk.

Your Forescribe,
Harriet

9

"Mom called," Dad told me over a cast-iron pot of black bean soup. "Said you never texted her back."

I shrugged in response. It was a loaded shrug, filled with anger and disappointment and frustration. To Dad, though, it likely seemed a regular shrug.

"She's busy," he said, rolling his eyes to his own words as if carrying on a conversation with himself. "I mean, hell, we're all busy. Look at that." He motioned to the large stack of ungraded papers near the exposed-brick fireplace. "Sixty-three essays in that stack. Not just sixty-three essays. No. Sixty-three pupils yearning to learn about Black America in its true form. One of those sixty-three students could run for president one day," he said. "You never know." He poked a spoonful of beans into his mouth to check the seasoning.

"And that one in sixty-three might just hide from their spouse that they're running for vice president. Yep. Spouse could find out while watching the nightly news, poor bastard." He glanced at me. "Sorry."

I wanted to tell him he was doing a phenomenal job, just as I wanted to praise Melody when she said my name. He rolled with it and that's all I or Melody or even Mom could expect under the circumstances. Guilt weighed on his shoulders. Guilt that they call a *mother's*, never a father's. But there it was, right in front of me.

A scroll flew through the mail slot. I saw it. Melody saw it. Dad didn't since his back was to the door. I got up, grabbed it, and hurried to the bathroom to read it.

"Sorry," he yelled after me. "I didn't mean to . . ."

And then it turned into a mumble that I couldn't make out. I wanted to know what he'd said, but this was the second scroll of the day. I sensed its importance and released some of my fear. As I unrolled it, it kept going and going like a CVS receipt. This letter was as long as I was tall.

I slid down the bathroom wall and sat cross-legged, settling into the thick green rug.

10

I've been writing all day. As I write
this, I sit surrounded by poems and
letters and sentences strewn here and
there, all around. I feel in a mania of
inscription and prose. I know myself well
enough to realize that I'm attempting to
write myself out of something challenging.
It's our way, you see? Dip into the ink
pot and fill the parchment. It can be
freedom, yes, but also, it can be a way of
avoidance.

    I tried mightily to circumvent
revealing to you, my Scribe, the brawl
happening within the depths of myself. In

letter 1, I hinted. In letter 2, I cued. In this one, Dear, I must strip down to my bare Black body. Fore I now realize it is the only way.

Ah, pain! There you are, old friend of mine. I can't mold you with my hands, oh pain, you will not allow that. You are here to be felt, and felt you are. I've been kicked, twisted, and taken against my will. But this pain is far worse than that.

The pain of a kick has a source. The twist of an already bruised wrist originates from an angry assailant. My spirit pushes out memories of my body taken by men who never deserved the opportunity to have it. But this pain, ah, yes. This is enough to make me regret being your Forescribe. Fore this is the pain of remembering a whole life. Sitting in it. Simmering. Melding decisions and regret. And allowing memory to run loops long enough to write it down so that you may understand me better. I wish it on no one. But alas, here we are.

I was born a slave.

That is the first line of my book.

I was born a slave.

Five words should not hold such power, so please allow me the opportunity to break them to bits.

I—Harriet Jacobs. A girl then. A woman then. A guide now. Forever a writer. A Scribe. A Mother. Ah, pain, there you are.

Was—It was so long ago. So, so very long ago. But what I was echoed through my children and their children and theirs and theirs, too. And now, my precious Black descendants hold on to pain for which they cannot adequately place the source. If what was hasn't been satisfactorily addressed, then was isn't was at all. Was is.

Born—My mother. My precious, precious mother. Through fire and fear, still she brought me forth. No enslaved woman should bear such a burden— bringing a baby girl into a world such as this. There is, in my opinion if you please, no greater power on earth than a mother.

A—Only a true Scribe knows the value of this letter added. Fore "A" means one of many. I didn't open my book with "I was born _the_ slave," now did I? I was not the only one. I was a speck within a mighty fleet.

Slave—Ah, pain.

Your pain is different than mine. This was my justification for not revealing myself in the very first letter. I've seen over many years the misguided comparing of pain as if one is worse or better. I've seen this with all people, here and far. It is a folly. A farce worth nothing more than a stroked ego or a scratched itch. Ah yes, I remember that feeling—an unreachable itch finally reached. It is enough to roll the eyes back and smile stupidly. I've seen that, too. Ecstasy. What a word that is, "ecstasy." So temporary, and too tempting for its own good. Word to the wise, dear Scribe, avoid it. I'm veering away from the truth, I fear. My apologies.

Ah, pain. _Slave_.

A Black girl in 1816 and a Black girl now are not comparable. They are, however, two sides of a rare golden coin that never made its way out of circulation. Scarred from too many transactions, this precious coin has earned a place on the mantel. Atop a silk pillow with fringe on the base. Yet, she still works her way through others' hands to get whatever it is they want from her that day. Through hands undeserving. Benefiting from her beauty, her delicacy, her will—so many do benefit, but so few respect. Rare she is, and rare she always has been. As you are, my Scribe, rare.

When I was a teenage Black girl like you, ah pain, I was a magical being. As I sit, eyes closed, remembering, I cannot summon words that do me justice. Just know, dear Scribe, that I was a gazelle trying very hard to hide in an open field. I failed at that.

Men and boys saw me, even as I veiled myself. The sun was so bright back then. Bright and hot and sizzling like a fried egg. To many, the sun was a sweaty spit but for me it was an unwanted spotlight. Damned sun clung clothing to my body. Cursed sun stuck long locks to the back of my exposed neck. Oh, that despicable sun made it impossible to hide.

Chased like an unbroken horse, I ran as long as I could within the confines of that plantation. I was young. Too young to understand that some men enjoy chasing. I was playing into his hands, fore his foreplay was breaking beautiful Black horses. In the midst, I ran into another man's arms. But this is not about men or boys or the intentional breaking of fragile things. No. This letter is to help you know your Forescribe. And to know your Forescribe, you must know what I love above all other things, even writing.

Ah, pain.

A Mother, in my opinion if you please, is the most powerful thing in the universe. When I was your age, I became one. And then again.

That's when I became breakable. Men noticed that to be the truth. They wanted me, and to get me fully, all they needed now to do was threaten them. So I blocked out the sun and hid in my grandmother's crouched crawl space for seven precious years.

I could not stand, ah pain. Nor lift my head. In the small space, I bent forward like a vulture and waited to glimpse my children playing in the yards. This is how you know you love something adequately. Through pain and loss of beauty and youth, a Mother loves like this.

Their names, if you would indulge me a moment to brag, were Joseph and Louisa Matilda. Ah worthy, treasured, beloved pain.

Dear Scribe: I fear I've made another purposeful admission. You are my first Scribe. I will make errors in judgment fore there is no guide for the guide. Do bear with me through and we'll forge a path together in the thick wilderness.

I must rest my mind. I will write again when I can. <u>Would that I had more ability! But my heart is so full, my pen is so weak!</u> Until then, pick up a pen of your own for goodness' sake.

Your Forescribe,
Harriet.

11

"Ah," I said aloud through a scratchy, unused throat. "Ah, pain."

A knock on the bathroom door shook me from my trance. "Okay in there?" asked my dad. "Sorry about before . . ."

I blinked a few rapid flutters to wet my dry eyes and then squeezed them shut to clear my head. As I rose, my knees crackled and I wondered how long I'd been sitting there. I'd been thinking of the letter, yet my mind felt empty somehow, like an about to be moved-in home with no occupants or boxes or anything at all.

"Didn't mean to offend," Dad continued, oblivious. "Got a little carried away . . ."

Harriet Jacobs was my Forescibe. There was no stalker or political saboteur. This was a formerly enslaved Black mother and writer when Black mothers were not allowed to write.

I was not losing my grip on reality at all; for some reason, reality was bending itself to bring me forward. I couldn't fathom why. I glanced into the bathroom mirror to search my eyes and nose and hair and cheeks for a specialness worthy of such magic. All I saw staring back at me was a regular girl. Quiet and odd, but nothing valuable. It was such a shocking and special thing to realize—a pen pal from heaven or wherever. A hero of a woman named Harriet sent to help me through.

Her first two letters felt like those free *Daily Bread* books at church—easily overlooked encouragements, the contents of which may change your life if you gave them a moment of seriousness, but no one ever did. After the third letter, though, something cracked open inside of me.

"It's just." Again, a knock. "I don't know what I'm doing here, and ..."

"Dad," I told him through the thick wooden door. "You're fine."

While he stayed silent, Melody interjected loudly and coherently for a one-year-old child. "Ruuuu! Oh! Ruuuuuu!"

I opened the bathroom door to find my dad's stunned hand frozen in the air like he was hailing a cab. I decided to give him a moment and crouched down to Melody.

"And you," I said, lifting her high into the air. "You're the smartest, wisest, most talented baby on earth."

"Ruuuu!"

"Good job, Baby," I told her. "You don't know how badly I've wanted to tell you good job."

I stood back to meet my father's eyes. "Now, tell me everything you know about Harriet Jacobs."

12

I held a dozing Melody as my dad poured hot water over handmade tea bags.

"She's a superhero," he said, more comfortable speaking about history than anything else.

I felt my eyes narrow in response and he saw.

"In what way is she a superhero, right?" he asked, leaning against the counter as the tea rested to steep. "My students ask that every time I teach Madam Harriet in 101, and this is my answer. When I was a boy, I thought my mother knew the future because she'd stop me from doing wrong before I even made the decision to act. *Every woman is thinking while you sleep*, she'd tell me. Just once, she added, *if you underestimate a thinking woman, it will be to your detriment*. You remember your G-Ma, right? She could turn a phrase, but that one I never let go. And when I first started researching Madam Harriet, I couldn't shake the thought that my mother was talking about her.

"Attempting to escape her captor and protect her children, she spent seven long years in a space not fit for a human body. So small and cramped that she couldn't lift her head or fully expand herself. She entered that unbearable space in her early twenties and it affected her life and health until she died at eighty-four."

Seemingly excited by what he was about to say, he abandoned the steeping tea and bounced to sit at the table next to Melody and me.

"But that's not what makes her super. I mean sure, seven years in a nightmare of a crawl space is some superhero-level stuff, too, but after the agony of the seven years, she wrote it!" He yelled the last three words so loudly that Melody stirred, and then he leaped to his feet to pace as he spoke.

"We had narratives from enslaved men. We had the brutality of slavery from the gaze of the enslaved *man*, you understand? Enter Madam Harriet! Woooo! She makes Superman look like an idiot flying around town in tights. This is a Black woman quietly blowing the lid off the bullshit. Exposing next-level agony of being a woman and girl enslaved.

"She wrote in *Incidents*, let me see if I can do her justice and quote . . ." He closed his eyes as if trying to remember her quote word for word. "'Slavery is terrible for men; but it is far more terrible for women. Superadded to the burden common to all, they have wrongs, and sufferings, and mortifications peculiarly their own.'

"Madam Harriet," he said, speaking to the ceiling. "If I messed that up, forgive me. She speaks candidly about the dimensions of sexual harassment, rape, manipulation—when no women could speak about those things. But she was Black. Imagine the nerve necessary to tell such truth!

"Madam Harriet lived in a time when Black women were not allowed autonomy over their own bodies. And somehow more horrible than that? The crippling threat of taking a woman's children as leverage. Men got to run away. Women had to stay and endure for the sake of their children. She is a knowing woman. A thinking one. A hero human being.

"I can't say this for sure," he said. "But I believe Madam Harriet planned her own life with pinpoint precision. Not like the rest of us plan; no, I believe she saw herself being seen by your eyes and mine. I believe she was resigned that her life would be one of unfathomable enslavement and running, maybe even her children's lives. A thinking woman to rule all the thinkers; even in that painful place, she thought forward to see what regular people could not see."

"What did she see?" I asked.

He smiled at my question as if grateful I'd spoken it aloud. "You."

He went over to pour the tea into two glass mugs. "Both

of you." He motioned to me and sleeping Melody. "And your mother, and . . . well. She knew there would be Black girls and women and she needed you to know her story for your own protection."

"What exactly is her story?" I asked, desperate to know details, but not wanting to read her book against her will.

He tilted his head in confusion. "What do you mean?"

Falling back into involuntary habit, I began counting the words in my response, not wanting to use too many. Thankfully, he continued speaking.

"I read *Incidents* to you and your sister when you were girls," he said, seemingly pained by the slight mention of Virginia. "Twice, actually. While every other kid in pre-K was hearing about little lambs being led around by Marys, you fell asleep to Madam Harriet's words. You really don't remember?"

Shadowy memories flashed in my mind but not enough to grab ahold of. When I shook my head, he slowly lowered his teacup and placed his head in his hands.

"Those moonlit nights were some of the best of my life," he said. "I should have read it a third time through so we could share those memories now. You were too young to stop at twice. I'm sorry."

I watched him for a while as he steeped like the tea, but in regret instead of water. Then, I had to ask.

"You speak about her in present tense," I said. "Why?"

He looked up with tears in his eyes and smiled through

them. "Because a woman like Madam Harriet never dies. She lives in her words. In her legacy. And, Ruth, in you. Madam Harriet was an underestimated woman, which I argue in my classes—all Black women and girls are. In her story, she proves my mother right. Her success and legacy are to the detriment of those who dared try to shut her up.

"Another of my mother's quotes that reminds me of Madam Harriet?" Dad perked up a bit speaking of his mother. "She once told my dad, *If I fall off a cliff, believe me, I'll get back up. If I'm pushed off a cliff, still believe I'll get back up. But I'll never forgive the muthafucka that pushed me.*" Dad laughed with such joy that I laughed, too. "Dad knew never to cross her. We all did."

13

In my dark bedroom later that night, train whistles shook me awake. Typically, the Birmingham trains were white noise to me, but something about this one broke through my dreamless dream.

As I sat there, straight backed and startled, the train screamed long, loud squeals, and then it moved along and my bedroom was left mostly quiet with the exception of Melody's sweet snoring on the floor by my bed. I knew I wouldn't be able to sleep, so I opened a new page in the notepad on my nightstand.

As I stared at the intimidating white page in front of me, my singular thought was of Virginia. That last morning when she looked back at me with large eyes and a charming grin. I thought of the triple knots in her shoelaces and wondered what stranger took them off that day—maybe a first responder or passerby.

I remembered the moment I found out what'd happened, on Twitter no less, there it was—*breaking*. I replied to that tweet and was bombarded with *rest in paradises* and condolences that I couldn't yet understand. Breaking. Social media forced mourning that I was not ready for. To find out, I had to search the platform with the keywords *Birmingham* and *Linn Park*. Virginia's face everywhere. Someone had already drawn her with angel wings and a halo. Virginia would've hated it. She'd call it cliché, ridiculous, empty; she'd always dismissed redundant breaking news.

Another train interrupted my memory and that's when I closed the notepad and placed it back on the nightstand.

"I'm not ready," I whispered. "Three words."

My voice seemed so different than I'd remembered it sounding a few months ago. Raspier and with more depth. Scratchy but not like a polyp, more like a phone sex operator from the Deep South.

Speaking in that moment made my heart ache. For some reason, to speak felt like an offense to my big sister's memory. Sort of like interrupting a moment of silence or speeding around a funeral procession on the freeway. I had no idea how long would be long enough to stay quiet. For Virginia, I could've done it forever.

But Harriet.

I'd been trying to push Harriet's third letter out of my

thoughts since talking to my dad. Her words inflicted real pain. They lashed and whipped, every one of them, as only words can. A true writer, Harriet Jacobs tapped the vein and drew blood on the page. *Ah, pain* was absolutely correct.

Also, she was right: If I was going to truly accept her as my Forescribe, I needed to know her. And if I didn't know her in that attic, I didn't know her at all. To top it all off, my dad's passion and understanding of her historical importance shook me in unexpected ways.

He revered Madam Harriet, as he'd called her. Honored her strength, resiliency, defiance. She seemed holy to him and I loved him more for it. But, simultaneously, he judged my mother, one of the most admired living Black women in the country, for her defiance and strength of will. She was a Black woman United States senator from Alabama, for goodness' sake. An undeniable badass. Was that level of reverence only reserved for dead Black women? Or was the inconvenience of being Mr. Mom too blinding for him to see clearly?

I pulled my knees into my chest and began to rock myself for comfort. I longed to join Melody on the floor by the bed, to be closer to her deep snores, such sweet whispers in the night. But I didn't want to wake her. Then it occurred to me, what if I was losing myself as Harriet had warned in letter two?

The notion that I'd so easily, wholly accepted a long-dead writer/mentor could in itself mean I was long gone.

Obsessively counting words certainly wasn't the sanest of behaviors, either.

I released my knees and crawled to Melody's side, giving in to my need for comfort. Her lips parted as she slept, forming the same O I recognized from our mother's face when she was about to dominate a lesser senator. Melody wore a sleeveless T-shirt revealing naturally toned arms. Her skin shone beautifully in a blue light. I looked around my room for the source of the light but I couldn't find it. Melody seemed to glow blue from the inside.

"Stunning," I whispered into the night. "One word and not nearly enough to describe such magic."

Black skin was exactly that, magic. What other explanation could there be?

I gently curled up next to her and fell asleep with her cocoa butter–scented hair centimeters from my nose.

14

At dawn, Melody screamed out so loudly I jumped to my feet. Her eyes fluttered as her tiny body shook so violently that I thought she might be having a seizure. I knelt back to her side and lifted her into my lap. When she calmed, I knew she'd had a horrible dream. Her large, terrified eyes locked with mine, and her tears streamed like a faucet.

"It was a dream, my precious girl." I rocked her back and forth on the floor. "A bad dream."

"Ruuuu," she said through a shaking stutter. "I wa-wa-wa-wa-wa . . ."

She lost the edge of her word and gave up on it entirely. I couldn't decide if I should push her to finish. Encourage her with clichés—you can do it, champ, don't give up, keep going. Or if I should just be with her—allowing her time to breathe. I went for the latter option.

"When you're ready," I said slowly and softly into her hair. "You tell me what you want. Until then, I want you to know something."

She twisted her body around to lock her precious eyes onto mine once again.

"If you line up every kid on this earth, and I mean every single one, I'd choose you every time to be my sister."

In response, she smiled and squared her shoulders as if forcing herself to get through the word. "I wa-wa-wa-wa-wa-wa-wa." She paused to see if I'd given up on her. I shook my head and smiled, happy to wait there all day long if it took that. "I . . . want . . . Mama."

And my heart shattered, right there on the floor by my bed.

"I know you do."

My phone was on the side table, so I called my mother on FaceTime before I had a chance to think myself out of it.

Her face popped up, openmouthed and ready to say a bunch of words. I knew from her expression that she was about to come up with a reason to get off the phone. I went straight for the heart with three words.

"Melody needs you."

"You talk?" she asked, genuinely astonished. "Your voice is . . . different."

I heard her aide in the background hurrying her along past inquisitive reporters. I caught sight of the US Capitol Building's columns and dome in the background. That's when I noticed her gorgeous white silk button down, definitely tailored. Her hair in a twist-out updo, pinned so beautifully there was no way she did it herself. And her makeup, flawless.

"Maaaaaa!" Melody yelled, grabbing the phone and halting my mother's hectic world.

She was crying still. Big tears pooled on her cheeks, refusing to drop. Melody kept petting the screen with her tiny index finger, trying hard to reach our mom. Every time, instead, Melody accidentally minimized her and wailed, setting loose the tears. The one on her left cheek reminded me of a snowball rolling down a hill and ultimately becoming large enough to take out a town.

This was not a bad dream of monsters or boogeymen. This was a child desperate to touch her mother's face.

"Ma'am. Ma'am. Ma'am. Ma'am. Ma'am . . ."

Background noise littered the call like seagulls barking on a beach. Melody was not pleased when my mother kept smiling at her crowd.

"Maaaaaa!!!!!"

Her one-year-old voice was louder than should be possible. I took the phone from her hands.

My next words were spoken with such force, I couldn't believe they were coming from me. "If you don't step away from those strangers and speak to your daughter right now, I swear I'll forget your name."

Twenty-one words. The harshest words I'd even spoken aloud to my mother.

"Ladies," Mom started. "Gentlemen. I need a moment."

"But, ma'am. Ma'am. Ma'am. Ma'am . . ."

And then her aide's green eye peaked over to see who was on the phone. "Ma'am," she chirped. "You don't have any spare moments today."

Mom smiled through bared teeth and I knew the look. I almost pitied the hell this poor chirping woman had to pay. Almost.

Smiling, Mom started in a quiet, but obviously pissed-off voice. "Excuse me, take no offense, but if you don't get the hell up out my face I swear 'fore God I'll make you."

"I didn't mean—"

"I didn't ask what you meant or didn't," Mom said, continuing to smile. "Back up while I speak to my crying child. And while you're at it, get these goddamn reporters back. Pull a rope from that pole to that pole so they can't damn near knock me down. In other words, do something other than ride my ass."

"Yes, but I don't have any rope."

My mom smiled again, tilting her head as I shook mine. *You don't have a rope,* I thought.

"You don't have a rope?" Mom asked, the disdain thick on her voice.

"I'll find one," she said before scurrying off. "I'll find one."

That's when my mother turned her full attention back to me. It'd been months since I had this much of her and a rush went through me because of it. This woman, my mother, had real power to change people's insides. I felt honored that she looked in my direction.

She smiled again, but not angrily. "You do sound different," she said. "You're growing up. Now, what's happening? And take as long as you need. They can't start without me, can they?"

She winked.

I stared at the screen for a few quiet seconds, trying to decide how many words this conversation would be worth. I couldn't remember this ever happening, her quieting herself to allow me to use up my words. Typically, her method was similar to what she'd done on *Lillian Tonight*—she dominated.

"Maaaaa." Melody interrupted my thoughts with her perfect little timing.

I looked into Melody's eyes and knew I wouldn't count my words this time. Melody couldn't speak. She needed someone to dictate for her, to express to her mother just how desperate she was to be near her. I lifted Melody onto the bed, curled her into my lap, and closed my eyes, forcing myself not to count.

"You left us," I told my mother, staring her in the eye without blinking.

"Well, technically, I—"

"No." I interrupted her, probably for the first time in my life. "You left us here after . . . You know, after . . ."

My mind went to counting and I took a breath to push the urge out.

"After Virginia died, you ran away as fast as you could." I tried not to pause but I couldn't help it. Pauses with my mother were dangerous invitations for her to speak, but she must've sensed the magnitude of the moment, because she didn't. She held the phone and watched me think it through. I appreciated that.

"I'm fine," I lied. "Stronger than ever before, but Melody is crumbling in my lap while you hop the United States in a red lip. I'm fine. Look at her."

I tilted the camera toward my lap to show my mother Melody's precious body curled tightly in my crossed legs. For some reason, Melody wasn't grasping for the phone like usual. She, too, was allowing me to express without interruption. I appreciated that, too.

"I'm fine," I said again. It was becoming a refrain and I knew that the more I said it, the less believable it was, but I couldn't stop myself.

"And Dad," I started. "Dad's . . . well. I don't know."

I felt myself going quiet again. My anxious mind blocked words. This is why I stopped speaking after Virginia's death. Anxiety had locked the gates and there was no way around.

And now I was taking up my mother's valuable time with uncomfortable silence.

"I'm fine," I said, shaking my head at myself. "I'll let you go, because yeah, I'm fine." I looked down at Melody to whisper, "I'm sorry."

"Can I?" she asked, and I nodded in response, not daring to look at the phone. I couldn't bear to see her disappointed eyes. I was the worthless daughter of a queen. Silent sister to the rising activist cut down too soon. She must've loathed my useless guts, no question. Surely she was thinking what I was thinking—I should've died that day, not Virginia.

"I'm so proud to be your mama," she told me in the same voice she used with Melody.

"This is not about me . . ."

"Ruth Fitz," she said with as much conviction as she did when arguing on the steps of the Capitol. "I'm so proud to be your mama."

"I'm fine, though . . ."

"You know why I named you Ruth?" she asked, unfazed. "I don't think I ever told you. Biblical Ruth gleaned the edges. Do you know what that means?" I shook my head and she continued. "She wasn't welcome in the already prosperous places, so they granted her the overgrown, desolate edge of her town. And with her hands, she transformed it into something so powerful and special that even those in the center traveled far and wide to set eyes on it. Ruth, my love, you watch. You wait. You hold tight to that which you are granted and one day, dear, you will glean it."

She closed her eyes and when she did, gold eye shadow glinted in the sunlight. "You'll be so much better than me," she said. "Right now, your voice is waiting in your gut to be put together like a puzzle on a coffee table. When it is, my God, you will be better than all of us."

"I'm . . ."

"Is anyone really fine right now?" she asked, smiling. "I'm certainly not fine."

That's when I looked at her, deeper than before. She smiled a smile of fabricated joy. It was a smile holding back floodgates so forceful it shook at the corners, ready to burst open. That was the smile of the saddest clown ever painted. She was not fine.

"None of us are fine," I replied with five words. Relief filled my body after I'd left so many words on the table, uncounted.

I saw a commotion happening behind my mother and my heart skipped a few beats. There she was—potentially the second most powerful human being on earth—standing alone in the bushes of Washington. She was a sitting duck and someone could pick her off as easily as they had with . . .

"Mom," I told her. "Get in the Capitol."

My mother smiled knowingly at my panic. "Calm down, Baby," she said with her phony expression back on.

"It's just the future president of the United States coming to fetch me."

"Well, well, well, Madam VP," said Jim Harrison. "Aren't you just a pile of where the heck are ya? We've been waiting for you."

My mother opened her arms and motioned him toward the phone. I sensed journalists in her orbit because she cleaned up her Alabama accent, trading it for something more generic. "Mothers everywhere, all over this country of ours, understand the necessity of stepping away from any and everything, no matter the consequence, to handle that which a father cannot adequately handle."

"Everything all right?" he asked with a strange-looking concern that, to me, looked more like irritation.

"Mama fixed it, just like I'll stand at your side as we fix this precious country." She winked.

"Ruth," he said, peering into my mother's screen. "I do sincerely apologize for taking so much of your mother's time. But I'm thrilled you'll be joining us on the trail next week, eh? We've got a bus full of all the bells and whistles just for you and your troop. Thing rides so smooth you'll think you're sleepin' in your own bed."

I stayed quiet and he looked around at what I assumed were reporters. "Mrs. Fitz's Ruth and my Judy are the same age. And I think they'll get along perfectly." I watched an epiphany walk across his face before he opened his mouth. "I have an idea! We'll be in Atlanta tomorrow. What say we send the big bus a few days early and we get the family merged? We can swoop you three up and get this party started."

My mother could not say no. There was no hesitating in front of reporters. I knew that. It would look like dissention. "Oh," she said, patting him on the back. "What a marvelous idea!"

Marvelous was not a word my mother used, ever. She was pissed off at the setup, and so was I. How the hell was I supposed to pack for a one-year-old? Not to mention the breast milk situation. That in and of itself would take planning, labeling, dating—tedious work for sure. This man had no idea how challenging it would be. Men had no idea. My mother, however, did.

"We'll send you, I don't know," she said, turning toward the presidential nominee. "What do you say, Jim, four of our assistants to help my Ruth prep for such an undertaking?"

I bit at my own smile. I envied my mother's verbal agility. I was uncomfortable at the thought of strangers in my personal space but grateful, because, yes, I needed help.

"Well, let's get on inside before the meeting's over," he said with an annoyed twitch in his brow. "And Ruth, whatever you need."

My mother winked at the phone and hung up. I lifted now-sleeping Melody onto my pillow and ran to the television in the living room to turn on MSNBC, and there she was—stunning, graceful, seemingly unaffected by the chaos around her. She waved and walked with the purpose of a stalking lioness. The logline underneath the Breaking News banner read "Presidential and VP candidates take meeting with House leadership."

I felt myself beaming. "My God," I said to the television. "My God," I said again. And my phone began lighting up with message after message about logistics of my new assistant's arrival. Her name was Jane. And her assistant's name was Harold. And then wardrobe was headed by Franny and Frank. And a nanny for Melody named Sunny. And they'd all be there this evening. All planning would take place on the private jet they'd already set up for tomorrow morning at BHM Airport, but what size was I and did I know what size my father was? And food, tell me about your food aesthetic. And I thought, what on earth was a food aesthetic? And Ruth, dear, you don't post many photos, do you? Are you a pencil skirt kind of second daughter or a flowy flowery second daughter? And Ruth! Hair! Braids? Micros? Anything you want, I'm happy to set that up right now. Atlanta has everything. We'll have hair and makeup in their own room at the hotel for your convenience. You'll need a tutor to keep up with school. What grade are you in . . . ?

It kept going. I hated text messages and emails. I never understood how people replied to them so quickly. It could take me a week to reply to a basic "how you doing" text. I'd read it and table it, then, seven days later, reply with I'm okay, and you? Texters didn't like that.

Dad's call broke through the text storm. "They've pulled my classes," he said calmly but devastated. "Looks like we're going on the trail whether we want to or not."

I glanced over the phone toward the television to catch sight of my gorgeous mother standing tight shouldered with the most powerful people on earth, the new Breaking News headline reading "In a rare move, House majority leadership officially endorses the Democratic candidates for the offices of president and VP."

"May as well embrace it," I told my dad. "Virginia would've."

His breath stopped. He wasn't expecting to hear her name and I certainly wasn't expecting to say it. It just came out. Nothing ever just came out of my mouth, but that did. In the corner of my eye, I saw a rolled scroll fly through the mail slot in the door. I ran to open the deadbolt and pulled the door open, but no one was in the hallway.

15

Dearest, Scribe:

I once planted a field of fruit trees in
a clearing around my grandmother's
residence. Actually, I cannot be sure if
seven trees can be called a field but to us,
it was. I was not quite a little girl when
I did the planting. I should have been
one still, but lengthy innocence, back then,
was a luxury held by white children and
not us.

I cultivated them from single seeds.
As I sit here writing, I almost feel them
in my fist, seemingly insignificant but

soon—to—be giants. Also, I recall laying
them out on a small wooden table.
Spacing them meticulously like soldiers
in a line. I watched them, always. First
as dry seeds. Then buried in cups of the
blackest dirt I could find. Then, dear
joy, after what I remember feeling like a
long time, new bright green babies broke the
surface. They lifted from the dirt, first
bowing to the new world and soon greeting
it with perfect posture.

Two pear and two persimmon and
two peach since they all longed for lifelong
mates to bear fruit. And then one apple,
who wanted to be alone.

I watched them every season.

The beautiful spring came; and when
Nature resumes her loveliness, the human
soul is apt to revive also.

I treated them like family should be
treated. I loved them and they loved me
so very much that they grew quickly,
bearing fruit within only a few years.

God saw me, you see? In my
sorrow, God reached into the dirt beneath
my feet and did the heavy lifting, only
requiring little from me. With water

77

and encouragement of words, the tiniest, quietest seeds fed many. I dare say, they still are doing that in the wild of what used to be my place of residence.

I have told you this story, my Scribe, because I have it on high authority that God, too, sees you. But you must give a little. He will, for you, do the heavy lifting but you must come to His table with at least a watering can.

What does your watering can look like? I can almost hear you asking as I write this letter to you. The answer, you will surely be disappointed to know, is up to you. Decide. Soon. Fore tomorrow, the plates will shift underneath your feet. Decide to embrace it as I did with those seven seeds. Embrace, dearest Scribe, the journey.

Your Forescribe,
Harriet

16

Jane showed up first thing in the morning. She was a hummingbird, flitting from front door to bedroom to kitchen to cupboard and back to the front door to let in Harold, her assistant.

"Harold, please take the secondary spreadsheet of must-brings and check them off as you find them. Fold, stack, label, index, and lay them out according to family member. You have six, no, five and a half hours before the luggage arrives, which better be on time since we are in a crunch. I've listed all necessary items according to perishability. Food's listed last, you see that, Harold? There will also be a Yeti filled with the crunchable ice for Melody. She's teething still, yes? Of course she is. They'd better arrive on time, or I swear. I don't know this company." Jane checked what I assume is her own master spreadsheet. "It's called Shippersaurus. Logo says they can ship anything within Birmingham in less than six hours. They'd better come through, so help me." She paused her flitting and turned to Harold. "Well? Go on."

And he did.

Jane muttered some more about checklists and Shippersaurus and private jets seemingly without taking a breath. I loved being around rare people like Jane. They alleviated all pressure for me to perform. I could sit in the midst and be, without worry of being the weird one who does not speak. I almost didn't mind her rummaging through my belongings as if she owned the place. Through cabinets and curios and freezer and . . . Almost.

"What's upstairs?" she asked with wide eyes.

"Nothing on your list," I replied with as much force as I could bring through my lips.

She went on rummaging. I slinked away and peeked in on napping Melody and made my way to the area upstairs I'd been actively avoiding. While trapped at home, I found comfort in knowing it was there—the upstairs. Dark browns and greens, rustic and smelling of books, even though I wasn't brave enough to venture up, it was close like an extra blanket if I absolutely needed it. But when Jane mentioned it, I realized I should go check up there before leaving.

Making my way up the steps, I heard Virginia's voice. I wasn't afraid of the sound, and the voice didn't say anything in particular. It was more of a hum, the beginning of a song, our song.

"Time" by Pink Floyd.

One night when we were very small, too small to under-stand Pink Floyd, we'd quietly made our way up the stairs with the flashlight smuggled from the emergency drawer and built a late-night fort in the center of the room.Virginia pressed play on an old cassette player in the corner. "Time" came on and we quietly listened to the instrumental intro-duction to a song that would become our favorite. It started with dings and chimes and pangs, then rose into a twisty-turny roller coaster of delicious weirdness. It was released in the early seventies as garage rock psychedelic mishmash music.We shouldn't have liked it; we fell madly in love with not only "Time" but the entire *Dark Side of the Moon* album.

But for whatever reason, we'd never shared our love with the outside world. Pink Floyd was our secret and no one else was privy to it. Sometimes, we'd walk the sidewalks of Birmingham—one earbud in my ear and the other in hers—sharing "Time." I thought of my dad the day before, with his head in his hands, remembering bedtime stories that no one alive remembered. No one to discuss one of the fondest memories of his life with, and I began to under-stand that sadness.What I wouldn't give to run downstairs and share "Time" with the only one who'd understand.

Then I heard it again, a hum of the first steady note

of our song. That's when I walked over to the old cassette player, still plugged in the wall where Virginia had left it, and pressed play. The ghostly hum was then met with the actual note and I wanted to close my eyes.

Instead, I began searching for the key to the locked antique writing desk. Virginia always knew it would turn up one day. She'd make a show of searching in the most ridiculous places like the inside of Easter eggs and in giant bags of Costco baby lima beans. She never found it, of course, but she never lost hope.

Something took over my body, an instinct to flit like Jane was doing downstairs, but what I felt bordered on frantic. I began by lifting couch cushions and throwing them to the floor. I fell to my knees and snaked along the wooden floorboards to see if the key had fallen in one of the deep crevices. And then, completely out of character, I began pulling the meticulously organized books from their comfortable shelves and shaking them out one by one as if the key might be a bookmark keeping a page. After, I threw each book aside until the room was wrecked. I then unrolled the stale yoga mats in the corner and threw them with all of my force. I would have screamed but I wasn't sure that my voice would be strong enough to handle it after so much silence. Afterward, I fell.

Surrounded by books and dust and what used to be beauty, I began to cry.

Our song was still playing. It was long, nearly seven

minutes, and it was on the part where there's what Virginia called a strange chorus of ahh's. I listened to the words as I had thousands of times before and cried for the first time in a long time.

Every year is getting shorter . . .

I began searching again for the missing key with a mania that matched the lyrics.

Never seem to find the time.

Then the words of the song dissolved into the air and I found myself pacing the cluttered floor. I was angry; lost like the key, and angry. And the song was making me madder.

"Quiet storm," I said aloud. "Two fucking words. Five words now! Eight! Nine!"

I thought of Virginia. She should be here holding my shaking hands until the frustration passed me by.

"Had to go to the goddamn protest," I said, competing with the crescendo of "Time." "Seventeen words!"

Then I thought of Dad hiding behind a well-manicured beard and beans.

"And you," I said before kicking a copy of *Gulliver's Travels*. "In such a hurry! You should've driven her there. Selfish!"

And I thought of Mom on her way back to DC as we lowered Virginia into the ground without her.

"Selfish!" I said with force. "Thirty-three words!"

I closed my eyes to see a quick vision of Melody toddling toward me. "Melody," I said quietly as I slid down the wall to a seated position. "Melody."

The lyrics to "Time" returned with the final bar.

The song is over, thought I'd something more to say.

It would've been the perfect moment to look over to my left or to my right and spot a golden key peeking through the newly destroyed room. I'd watched enough movies to know that was the moment when the thing showed up. The music coming to a head, rising and rising until the main characters bounced up and spotted the previously lost item lying there as if a grip or prop manager had placed it there for that very moment.

This was that moment for me.

I looked left. And then I looked right. And then forward and then behind me. No key.

"Fuck."

I threw a book at the cassette player and it fell on the hard floor and burst to silence. A ring at the door broke through it accompanied by Melody's cries. I dried my wet face, lifted myself up, and went downstairs to find that Jane had already let in the wardrobe team—Franny and Frank—who were wheeling in three packed racks of clothing. Sunny, Melody's nanny, brought up the rear.

Franny air-kissed both sides of my face and Frank did the same.

"I'm Franny."

"And I'm Franky."

Overwhelmed, I studied them. They were not at all what I would've imagined a wardrobe team called Franny and

Franky would look like. No uninterrupted black leather or attitude to speak of. They were, instead, dressed for utility. Franny wore oversize blue jean overalls with many pockets, all of them seemingly full, while Franky wore a basic white T-shirt and cotton drawstring pants, also with filled pockets.

"She doesn't say much," Jane said. "I've checked out her closet and her aesthetic is, I don't know, not really there. The husband's visuals, though, exactly what you'd guessed they were, Franny. He's African American history professor chic. Handsome man, thank goodness." As she spoke, Jane looked through Dad's rack of clothing, nodding approvingly. "Yes, this will do. He'll look mighty fine standing next to Madam Vice President in this number."

Jane was doing her job, I told myself. But it was hard not to be angry at her referring to my accomplished, revered, brilliant father as "mighty fine."

"Hi," said Sunny, who'd been hanging in the back. "I'm the nanny. May I?" She held her arms out for Melody to fall into.

Instinct twisted my stomach and made me hold on tighter to Melody, but my baby sister smiled and leaned forward comfortably into Sunny's arms as if telling me it was okay to her let go. Sunny looked not yet middle-aged but not fresh out of college, either. In between the two, gentle and kind. She wore a PUBLIC RADIO NERD T-shirt and soft, well-worn jeans. She quickly swept Melody into the next room to play with magnet blocks on the floor, and relief came over me as I watched them. Melody was pure joy. I loved her more than anyone else in the world, but she was a full-time responsibility and I was grateful for the help.

"Honey?" asked Jane. I had no idea she'd been talking to me. Honey was not my name. I turned around to face her. "Can you explain your style to Franny and Frank? Okay," she continued. "If you don't feel up to trying to explain, just go to your rack and choose three items that make sense to you. They can go from there."

Franny and Frank nodded along warmly as I took a few steps toward the rack with my name on it. Half of the clothing selections were pink. There were many tailored suits in the mix and a few flowing dresses with flowers. No brown, no black, no gray, which was, as they say, my aesthetic.

I turned to look at them for encouragement. They just stared back, waiting. So I closed my eyes and randomly chose three things off the rack—a pink tea-length dress, a long-sleeved flowery chiffon blouse, and a bright yellow suit. I went to put all three items back but they were swiped from my hands before I had the chance.

Franny and Franky immediately went to empty their pockets of pins and needles and threads of many colors. Franny even pulled out a contraption that looked like a fork with color balls attached to the sharp tips. I couldn't imagine what it was for but she laid it out with such care that it had to be important.

"Strip," said Franky without an ounce of hesitation, as if he asked the Uber driver to strip the exact same way.

"No," I replied, and all three of them stopped their busy hands. "I'd rather in the bathroom, if that's okay."

Nine words. And three of them—*if that's okay*—hurt badly. That was a piece of my personality that I hated more than any other. The piece that apologized for existing in the first place. *If that's okay* meant I didn't want to offend a total stranger who'd just asked me to take my clothes off. I hated myself. I felt tears coming and I wanted to hide. Then, a small, sweet tug at my ankle, Melody.

"Ginia . . . Ma . . . Dadada . . . Ruuuuuuu!" she stuttered through.

I lifted her in my arms and stared into her precious eyes.

"You got it, Baby."

She stared back without the words, but her eyes said "You got it, too."

I turned to the three of them and said, "I don't know any of you well enough to change clothes in front of. I will not strip. How can you do what needs to be done without me stripping?"

"Ruuuuuuuu!"

17

Later that evening, Dad walked in with more donuts and a six-pack. He went to hide the beer behind his back but it was too late, he'd seen the shock in my eyes. I had no idea he drank alcohol. Disheveled and uncharacteristically confused, he scurried to his room and came back empty-handed.

"How did you all get that monstrosity of a bus here so fast?" Dad asked with a bit of a slur. He outstretched his hands so awkwardly that I wanted to pull at his skin to make sure he wasn't an imposter.

Jane stopped and stood still for longer than she had the entire time she'd been in my home. "Sir," she began. "Your wife pulled every string imaginable to get that monstrosity here so that you and your children may be as comfortable as possible."

"Well then," he replied. "I suppose I should call and thank her for her unimaginable string-pulling powers. What is your name anyway?"

"Jane. I'm here as your personal assistant."

"You're here to do anything I ask?" he asked more rudely than I could've imagined.

"Anything your wife asks, actually," Jane said firmly. "The future vice president of the United States."

"Ah, yes, well," he said. "We'll see."

"I think it may be a good idea if you go lie down a while," Jane said to him. I wouldn't have imagined a stranger talking to my father that way in his own home. "We're handling things nicely out here for now, thank you."

To my surprise, he obliged, disappearing into his room and closing the door.

"Not so handsome after all, is he?" asked Franny.

"No," replied Franky and Jane in unison.

I wanted to protest on his behalf, but they were not wrong. I'd never seen my father like that and if I was meeting him for the first time, I'd think the same or worse. He was a mess.

We heard a crash come from his room. "I'm okay!" he yelled behind the closed door.

"This typical of him?" Jane asked me with creases of

concern between her eyebrows. "No offense, but that's a problem."

I shook my head. No words should be wasted on trying to defend such behavior.

"I'll have to let Mr. Harrison know before we take off tomorrow morning," Jane said, taking out her cell phone to text with the fastest thumbs I'd ever seen. "He won't like it, that's for sure."

I cringed at the memory of my dad and Mr. Harrison's already salty relationship on those video calls. This would give Mr. Harrison more reason to loathe my usually loveable father.

I wondered what had pushed him over the edge. I assumed, knowing my dad, that it was the loss of his history classes. That was a point of real passion for him and maybe, in the midst of my mother and the demands of politics, gave him something tangible and honorable to hold on to. Otherwise, he might float away into a fog of loss and pain and unending parental responsibilities. But then, he could have been thinking of Virginia. Or the shifting of marital roles before his very eyes. Or, it could have been old-fashioned, green-eyed jealousy.

I'd never even thought of my father as a jealous man. Back when we'd go places as a family, he'd be introduced as distinguished. Plaques and awards covered the white walls of his office. He topped every list of Black men doing big things in the Southeast. He organized marches and gatherings and scholarship lunches for young professionals. He was swarmed when he entered rooms and he usually bowed his head like it embarrassed him to be the center of attention.

That I found especially charming. I hated when people drank praise like sweet tea, something I'd seen in many men in Birmingham. I'd once seen the former mayor hold his arms open like a savior while the audience stood and clapped. My father was the opposite. He stared at his feet as others spouted out his accomplishments and I loved him more for it. But now, the more I thought of it, he truly might have been jealous of my mom.

No one cared about his classes or scholarship lunches anymore. At least, no one in our periphery.

Logic says he'd be proud of her. The doors would open not only for her but for him, too. He could teach anywhere in the world now. Long-game strategy was win the goddamn election and all of our tickets would be written in whatever ink on whatever parchment we wanted. As I thought more and more of my father, drunk and stumbling like a fool, I couldn't stop myself from confronting him. I stormed to his door and knocked, hard.

"Come in," said a small voice that didn't sound at all like my dad.

When I opened the door, the air left my lungs. He'd brought down all of the yoga mats from upstairs and unrolled them onto his bedroom floor. He'd placed the beer on one mat and the donuts on another as if they were yoga partners.

He was on another in child's pose, crying. I quietly moved the remaining four beers from the six pack and joined him in child's pose. We were facing each other.

In yoga classes I'd taken in the past, I always had the foresight to take the spot closest to the wall. That way, during child's pose, I wouldn't have to awkwardly face anyone. But there we were, father and daughter, silently peeking at each other from underneath our armpits.

"You destroyed the upstairs," he whispered. "I get it."

"You bought donuts," I replied. "I get that, too."

We laughed together for the first time in a long time and it felt so good.

He rose into downward dog and so did I. That also felt so good. The long stretch in my arms, stiff from holding Melody in the wrap. The almost pain in my lower back. Even my face. Gravity forcing my cheeks into a smile I thought I'd lost. I'd forgotten the power of short yoga poses. After a few moments, he flowed into a sun salutation and then took a seat, straight backed and legs crossed. And so did I, facing him.

"We should do yoga more often," he said, still slurring but not horribly. "Might just help."

I nodded.

"I was rude out there, huh?"

I nodded.

"Scale of one to ten?"

I held up all ten fingers.

"I need to apologize."

I nodded.

"First," he started. "To you. You've been more the parent lately than I have. To Melody and to yourself. I am sorry."

He got up to leave the room, stumbled, and stopped. "Should I do it tomorrow?"

I nodded and closed the door behind me as he crawled into bed.

18

The night was a long one without Melody sleeping on the floor next to me. Sunny had gotten her down in her crib and I kept getting up to check in on her. Every time I went into her room, I expected my Melody to be awake with her tiny arms raised for me to swoop her up, but she seemed content there and I felt a pit of sorrow growing in my stomach.

Change, I realized, was coming.

I went to the kitchen to make sure Jane had gotten the frozen milk stash, and found that she'd not only emptied the contents of the freezer but the refrigerator, too. And scrubbed it spotless.

At the sight of the barren refrigerator, I wondered exactly how long we'd be gone. From the looks of it, they were planning for the long haul. Maybe even a four-year-long term.

I sat in the armchair closest to the front window. Dad was right, the tour bus was enormous. Large enough to take ten spaces in front of our building. And Mr. Harrison's hokey face smiled up at me from the side of the bus. Mom's must've been on the other side facing the street. In the photograph, Mr. Harrison looked like he wanted to wink. He was the opposite of my mother—always putting on and showing large teeth. My mother, however, was stingy to smile and called horrible names for it. They truly belonged on different sides of that bus.

My mother's more cordial colleagues referred to her as rigid. The less cordial ones called her a bitch. One was even caught on camera doing so. I raged on the inside when I saw the viral clip. At first, my heart broke for her—millions of people viewing such a moment—but my broken heart was unfounded. She took what would've been embarrassing to anyone else and flipped it into an opportunity to book every show on television.

I watched her evening after evening, even some mornings, on the news. She never lowered her chin when they played and replayed the moment a square-jawed South Carolinian representative spewed that vile insult at her in the halls of the Capitol. I stared at her chin every time, examining it. Studying it. Envying it.

Sometimes, when I was alone, I'd pause that moment

and squat down to my knees to position myself next to the frozen image of my confident mother. Then, I'd slide out the hand mirror hidden underneath the console and lift my chin to match hers.

We looked alike in the nose and the eyes and cheekbones. Even our jaws were similar in shape. I'd found an old high school yearbook a while ago, and back then, my mother looked exactly like I do now. She spat me out, as my grandmother had said before she passed.

But there, side by side, me real and her frozen on internationally televised news, our similarities were on the surface only. I looked like her, yes, but my chin rested naturally on my chest, bowed, while hers lifted toward the sky, unaffected even by the most powerful of men.

I wanted so badly to be like my mother. And I knew that I wasn't alone in that desire. The whole world was in her shadow, whereas before it had just been me. I looked down at the bus again. The potential president's teeth were so white they practically glowed in the near dark. He, too, was in my mother's shadow and I wondered if he realized it. He was at the top of the ticket, but in comparison to my mother, he was a regular dude. She was the star of this show and she deserved both sides of the bus.

Sitting there in the wee hours before the biggest move of my life, I allowed myself to react to my father's behavior. I closed my eyes and stilled my thoughts, trying hard to identify how I felt about it. The only word I could come up with was *disappointment*.

I wanted to be like my mother, but my father was the coolest human being I'd ever known. He stayed calm when the world was chaotic. He marched the streets of Birmingham alone in loafers until someone, anyone, paid attention. He taught with the passion of a man born to never stop learning. He wore suspenders instead of belts, deep V-neck button-down sweater vests, and sported a neat manicured beard.

His spare time was spent growing vegetables for his family to eat and clipping at his many finicky Bonsai like they were his children. He lived life like I would one day choose to live life, with care and purpose, never focusing on the frivolous. But then, my mother took her rightful place in the spotlight. No one, not even him, could deny that she belonged there. But when she did, he turned into something unrecognizable—a jealous, resentful husband.

After Virginia . . .

I thought he was grieving. I assumed the changes were side effects of the unspeakable pain of losing the light of his life. I felt it, too. But every day, it was becoming clearer that this was not grief. Or maybe, this was some weird mashup of grief and jealousy. Or maybe, worse so, it was the grief and jealousy, and the latent chauvinism of a man not wanting to be outdone by a woman.

I squeezed my eyes shut. Even thinking it felt like a betrayal to the man I thought my father was. How dare I imagine it? But there it was.

There it was.

My father was well known throughout Birmingham. He'd taken it over as his own, marching, teaching, speaking, mentoring, smiling, and leading a generation of Central Alabama youth. Up the I-59 corridor, down I-20 East and West, clear toward Leeds and around Fountain Height and Druid Hills, ask anybody his name, Joseph Fitz, they all knew. And they spoke of him fondly.

I couldn't see it then, how much joy he gained from being the most popular member of the family. I just thought he was a happy-go-lucky guy and phenomenal, selfless human being. Until my mother effectively implied he could have Birmingham as she went on to take over the world.

I continued to sit at the window, staring at Birmingham as the rising sun began to turn the horizon a burnt orange. Over the bus and buildings, into the distance toward Dynamite Hill, I watched my city. Bravery met hatred in Birmingham. Bull Connor, KKK, and other terrorists rode up and down Center Street with threats and bombs and bullets. The magic city, they call it. A tear fell down my cheek and onto my forearm.

I couldn't figure out if I was crying about my father or my mother or Virginia or Melody sleeping in her crib for the very first time. But something about the sunrise over the city I'd grown up in made my stomach twist like a wrung washcloth. My chin began to jump and I was truly, undeniably crying.

That's when Melody began to scream my name in her sleep. I leaped to her room, glad she hadn't replaced my name with Sunny's just yet. I cradled her to the foot of my bed where we both fell asleep sprawled on the floor.

19

This time, I woke up with the scroll on my chest. And ...Yes! It scared the crap out of me!

Dearest, Scribe:

A Black father—not unlike a Black mother, but somehow, not at all like a Black mother at the same time—has always been a brave thing to be too, my love.

I loved mine. As long as I had him and long after I'd lost him, I longed for him. I fear there will be much longing in this letter. You, Scribe, will know as I do that sometimes one does not realize what she longs for until she places pen to parchment. Ah, longing.

We are the luckiest of them all, dearest. Blessed with Fathers who would proudly take the brunt of the hit so we would never have to. To be born a girl with a Father deserving of an uppercased F. Ah, sweet longing for the protection of such a rare being.

The best of them possess an innate instinct to protect, as mine did. He stands, arms spread like the wings of an eagle, in the gap between the cruel world and the face of his daughter. The best will not stray from the loving wife of his youth. Be honest, dear Scribe, we judge those who do. Harshly.

I've witnessed fathers unworthy of daughters and the unfailing love of first wives. I've known a father to slam a rickety door in the face of his frail wife, only days after she had given birth to his daughter. All for the fleeting compliments of his crying mistress. That mistress quickly turned on him after he walked away from his family. Foolish fathers have no right to call themselves fathers.

The saddest twist in that saga, dearest, was not the downfall of the father himself fore he earned that. But the forever longing of his baby girl. Ah, uncontrollable, unreasonable longing. She wrote like us. No. She wrote nothing like us. She wrote into her bleeding forearms—P.A.I.N. She wrote to feel. To fill. To hurt herself. To make herself hurt. She drew poetry into herself until, one day, she cut too deep. Ah, excruciating, acute, razor—sharp longing.

But my Father was polar opposite of that.

I was born a slave; but I never knew it till six years of happy childhood had passed away.

My Father played a large part in that happiness.

Our Fathers, dear Scribe, have thus far proven to be better than this. I write carefully here, because I understand that yours has lost his way of late. I, too, understand that you hurt because of it. So, allow me a few paragraphs of a story:

My Mother (now that I realize the honor of uppercasing, please allow me to

honor also my Mother) used to tell me
a small story about my large Father.
She'd said, one day, she'd noticed water
collecting at the corner of the place we
called home. She told me, in the chaos of
the day's chores and children, she'd forget
that it was there and would step in it at
least once per day.

She'd then say, every time she cursed
and yelled to herself shaking her wet foot,
my Father's laugh would echo through
the yard. And his laugh made her laugh.
I can remember his laugh—the shoulder—
shaking sort—was quite contagious.

Around that time, she'd tell me, she
recalled him tinkering with small batches
of sticks and twigs in what little spare
time he had. The bendable kind that take
braids without snapping. At this point in
the story, my precious Mother would often
pause to stop herself from crying. She was
such a strong woman. Powerful in her
quiet focus on the most important things
and nothing else. She'd dab at her cheeks
and then take a small breath to continue.

One summer day, she turned that
familiar corner at the back of the house,

likely running after me or my brother, and stepped on the wet spot to find her foot dry and steady on a solid surface. She looked down to see that her husband, my Father, had braided for her the most beautiful little bridge. He'd woven some of the thinnest switches she'd ever seen until they were stronger than bricks. He could've simply plopped a large rock in the wet spot, she'd tell me. That would've done the trick just fine, but he took weeks to sift the woods, collect the best, and build something worthy of a wife so worthy.

I listened to my Mother tell that story dozens of times as if I hadn't helped him search for all those hard-to-find switches. We walked the wood—my Father and me—for days and days. We climbed tall trees to unwrap the clingiest ones from limbs. Together, we braided a bridge for my precious Mother to cross. That's the Father I had, albeit briefly. I had him.

I do not tell you this to boast. Quite the opposite, I tell you this so that you may understand the power a Father has over his girl. Fathers (Fathers) understand this, deep on the inside.

Fathers (fathers) do not understand until it is too late—their daughter has grown and married a rascal similar to the rascal he showed her in himself.

The power of a Father means I recall this interaction hundreds of years later. This tiny gesture of love between my parents means so much to me that it transcends time and space. I remember it as if it were yesterday. My Mother likely understood the weight of that moment. That would explain why she repeated the story so many times, but my Father didn't realize the power of what he'd done.

It is, my Scribe, one of my few regrets, that I did not help him understand his power. I was young, too young to possess the adequate words, but I longed for him to know then as I long for him to know now, though he's dead and gone. Ah, irrational longing of a daughter for her Father.

I tell you, Scribe, remind yours of his power.

I sincerely apologize for asking this of you because, alas, this is not your job.

If I could, I'd send him a scroll of his own. I cannot. I am not his Scribe. I am yours.

Tell him.

While he still has a capital I.

You must use your voice. I know this is not easy but you have to speak your truth. Or, if you please, _write_ your truth.

I will end with this.

Too many fathers possess egos too large to bend. They are fragile, you see? Like regular sticks lying in plain sight in the woods. But Fathers like ours, dear Scribe, are tangled tightly, high up in the limbs of the tree canopy. And sometimes, they need their daughters to climb carefully up and up to unwrap their stubborn vines.

Your Forescribe,
Harriet

"Up, up, up!" Jane chirped as she burst into my bedroom without knocking. She drew open the closed curtains to reveal the full Alabama sun. "Sunny, come get the baby ready. Franny, Frank? Bring the cream suit for Ruth."

Sunny lifted Melody's still sleepy body from my lap and

I felt my forehead squeeze in confusion. Jane definitely noticed.

"I know we didn't pick out a cream suit yesterday, but trust me, it's necessary for the jet. Those regular clothes will work fine for the bus, but this is your debut," she said as if trying to convince a toddler to eat broccoli. "It's stunning. It's the first time the public will see you as a family. I'll give you five bucks?"

"Say five hundred," Frank whispered into my ear as Jane shot him a look. "What? You're good for it."

"Your mother will wear a fiery red pants suit," Jane said as she wheeled in a cart with an expensive-looking hanging bag, three shoeboxes, and a tray of wigs and makeup. "Sweet Melody will wear a navy blue striped dress. Your father will wear a navy suit with a perfectly matched red tie. And you, well, you'll wear cream."

Jane held her hands together, thumbs touching and forming a frame. "Perfect family walking down the stairs of the private jet, one by one. Your mother will hold Melody, of course. I'm telling you, the aesthetic will drop jaws."

I saw it. I wasn't completely void of vision, and of course, she was correct. The nation would set eyes on us and see a well-dressed, patriotically coordinated family ready to walk into the White House. An introduction such as that got votes, and my mother wanted to win, badly. Still, I deliberately held my expression from Jane until she reached into her pocket and pulled out a wad of hundreds.

"Fine," she said, fanning out five hundred-dollar bills in my face. "Fake it?"

I caught a whiff of the bills. My instinct was to reject them. Be above bribery, Ruth, you're better than this. But this was not about personal morality. My life was being flipped upside down. Not only mine, actually, Melody's, too. The contents of our categorized refrigerator had gone. My father's beloved career eliminated in an afternoon. Our whole world spun. And it had all been done by a group of people we'd only just met. What if something happened and I needed to whisk my baby sister away? I couldn't very well do that with my current checking account balance of thirty-three dollars and seventy cents. I took the money with a knot in my stomach.

"Extra hundred for a ruby-red lip," Jane added with a wink.

20

They'd intentionally rotated the chair away from the mirror, so I had no clue what I looked like, but I knew I wouldn't like it. I cringed at the thought of being made over; still, I let them do it. All of it, cream suit, red pumps, even the red lip and shoulder-length wig with blink-away, layered bangs.

I'd never worn a wig before. It hadn't as much as crossed my mind to wear one. Usually, I gathered my wet, natural curls to the top of my head until they dried down into a small puff. If I was feeling fancy, which I rarely ever did, I'd throw a bandanna around it. Honestly, I'd never given much thought to hair or clothing or makeup or anything like that, and thankfully, no one in my home cared in the least. They all accepted me, even on my unkempt days.

Virginia especially. She'd cross the threshold into our bedroom and shed all of what made her popular at school and online. Out there, she was power and grace and activism. But alone with me, she was torn jeans and books and open ears and relentless encouragement.

I'd known sisters at school who seemed to hate each other, never missing an opportunity to tease each other publicly. That, I never understood. Real enemies exist in the world, especially in high school, so to fight one's own blood feels wholly counterintuitive. Virginia and I were the opposite of those sisters. We were pure sibling love on full display, no matter who watched.

We fought, too, but only in private. I tried not to remember those fights, since they were all my fault. Virginia hung out with friends I didn't approve of. They took risks that I wouldn't dream of taking, and I judged her for it.

She never judged me for being an uncombed homebody, but I rode her constantly about her risk taking. Looking back, they weren't really even risks. She was a free spirit, not a troublemaker. I should have trusted her just like she'd trusted me. Still, I did it—questioned her whereabouts and social media posts, even her outfits. I should have let her live as long as she could.

Ah, pain. There you are.

"What on earth are you thinking of, Ruth?" asked Jane. "You're a million miles away."

I shrugged at the question.

"Well," said Franny, holding tight to my shoulders. "Are you ready to see yourself?"

Frank and Jane stood over me like seagulls would a crab, grinning and ready to peck. Again, I shrugged.

The spin of the chair was a slow, dramatic one. As I spun, I took in my living room, then the hallway leading to mine and my father's bedrooms, then the refrigerator, and then the kitchen cabinets, until I saw someone who looked a little like me except that she was hiding behind a lot of extra stuff.

She looked like a silent girl trying to be a vocal woman. She looked like a thousand-dollar wig in a ten-thousand-dollar suit. And there was the red lip. She looked like a pageant contestant ready to answer a question regarding world peace. She looked like a successful job interview. She looked like a girl with six hundred dollars cash in her sweaty palm. She looked a little bit like her mom, but kind of like her dad, too, and her sister Virginia somewhat with a hint of the baby, Melody. She looked like the well-packaged daughter of the future vice president of the United States. She looked like a winner in every conventional sense.

I caught myself peeking around her every now and then. Through strands of slightly tinted bangs where I hid. Underneath strategically placed lashes, I blinked away the blur of whoever the hell that girl was and tried to find myself. I squinted hard and there I was, disguised in things I would never have voluntarily sought out.

"One more thing," Franny said as she lifted a necklace around me and fastened the clasp. "I had it made specially for you."

It was solid gold and the inscription read "Quiet Storm."

I stared at the intricate engraving. It wasn't the twenty-dollar kind from the middle of the mall. This was perfectly scratched and chiseled gold that reminded me of Middle Earth. I locked eyes with Franny and felt myself trying not to cry. "How?" I asked, and they all looked pleased with themselves.

"Your mother told us that was Virginia's nickname for you," said Frank in a low, deliberate tone. "I hope we didn't overstep."

"Thank you," I told him.

Somber entered the room like a funeral. I looked to Frank and then back to Franny and I could tell they had no idea what to say. People, in general, didn't know and that was all right. But since Virginia . . . I'd observed the knee-jerk response was this—a subdued, dismal gloom that felt a bit like respect. Also, though, it felt like an uncontrollable instinct to get the hell away from the girl who lost her sister. Like sibling death was catching or that it might rub off on anyone in my vicinity.

"I knew you'd love it!" said Jane, thankfully not giving into the melancholy around her. "I told you! Didn't I tell you? You look like a star. No, you *are* a star. Full stop.

Now . . ." Jane paused. "Let's go work on your father, if he's even awake."

As they scurried off toward my father's room, I reached for the necklace, and in the process, accidentally dropped the six hundred dollars Jane had given me to become . . . this.

Quiet storm.

I felt it, rising inside of me—a storm but not so quiet. Something powerful brewed in my gut and I couldn't meditate it away or extinguish it like I usually did. I wanted, more than anything, to peel this layer of someone else away and write. I wanted to do what Harriet told me to do and place pen to parchment so that I might set myself free.

Free from my beloved sister whose hold seemed to tighten more and more every day. Her grip like chains on my wrists. A grief unaddressed. A pain unattended. Her memory so fond, but also, months later, something heavy, weighing me down. Preventing me from placing one foot in front of the other so that I might move on with my life.

Free from the weight of family. All of them, even Melody, if I'm honest, were heavy.

Free from this goddamn wig.

Free from this ruby-red lip.

Free from my very first ride on a private jet.

Free from the photo op of walking down the steps, gripping rails, and waving for the snap, snap, snaps of ABC and NBC and CNN and FOX and all of them.

Free to do what I wanted to do. Which, as Harriet understood, was to write.

I brushed my fingertips over the letters in my new necklace and felt guilty.

One by one, I picked up the damp hundred-dollar bills from the kitchen floor and made my way downstairs to the street. As soon as I exited the building, an SUV skidded to a stop and I had no idea why. The driver rolled down the passenger's side window and leaned toward me.

"Hey," he said, smiling like an idiot. "What's your name?"

I shrugged at the question and the fact that he started driving as slowly as I was walking while a line of cars waited behind him. Some passed around, honking their horns angrily, and others flailed arms in frustration. I'd never witnessed such blatant disregard from a driver.

"You hard of hearing?" he asked, proudly flashing an empty space where a front tooth should've been. "I said, what's your name?"

The chaotic honks behind him finally reached a fever pitch and he sped off, but not before calling me a Black bitch.

At first, I walked as fast as I could in the pumps, until I quickly realized how painful pumps actually are. *Why would anyone do this?* I thought. *What's the reward for such a needling?* I got my answer.

Honks. All around me, honks and whistles and dropped

jaws. I tried to duck into a Subway but there was no hiding in red heels and a cream suit. In that moment, I remembered Harriet describing herself as a gazelle attempting to hide in an open field. I'd never been there until this very moment. Uncomfortable wasn't the right word for what I felt. I couldn't think of what the right word was. Maybe there wasn't one. It was a mixture of flattery and pride and gratitude and absolute horror and vulnerability and shock and power.

That's right, there is no singular word for it.

I hurried back to my building and, once inside, locked the door behind me, only to find myself face-to-face with my father in a tailored blue suit, meticulous red tie, and very expensive-looking shoes so shiny I could've seen my new self in them.

"My God," he said, staring at me like I was someone else. "You look . . . My God."

My head lowered as it did when I felt uneasy.

"I mean," he continued. "You've always been beautiful. You were born beautiful, but . . . My God."

"Ruuuuu!"

I nearly twisted my ankle to get away from my father and to Melody's side.

"You're a doll, Mel," I told her. "An absolute doll."

Melody smiled with all seven of her teeth and grabbed a tight hold of my new necklace as if she knew how much the two words written meant—*Quiet Storm*. She studied them and her eyes sparkled. Her hair had been braided up into a ballerina knot at the top of her head and her dress was a poufy, navy-blue striped showstopper. Ribbons flowed from the back of her waist and hair and even from her shoes. She positively glowed.

"You're the most beautiful girl in the whole world, Mel," I said, lifting her into my arms. "And it's not even close."

Franny, Frank, and Jane gathered in front of us with proud expressions all around.

"This," Jane started. "Is a picture-perfect second family of the United States." She glanced at her watch and did a little jump on her heels. "We're seventeen minutes behind schedule! Car's downstairs, everybody out!"

"But aren't we taking the bus?" asked Dad. "That monstrosity is taking up space out front. Who's paying for the meters? Not me. And I have the mayor on speed dial. You will not make me look bad in front of the mayor for unpaid parking tickets. Not on my watch."

Jane stood more still than I thought she could, seemingly waiting for my father to stop his ridiculous tirade about nothing at all.

"Are you done?" she asked, obviously about to obliterate him. "Your wonderful wife, the future vice president of the United States, has already been in contact with that mayor you have on speed dial. She has, in fact, offered him a position in her cabinet. Parking should not be an issue, sir. Any more concerns? Questions?"

My father didn't answer. He, instead, looked away.

"Good, then," she said. "Let's go! Before we miss our own private jet."

21

Making one's way through the Birmingham airport is tedious. I'd always loathed check-in, and bag drop and TSA and gate checks and bag pickup and everything else. It made me claustrophobic. In the car ride over, I closed my eyes attempting to prepare myself for the chaos, but when I opened them, there was none. Instead, there was a private, gated entrance where a concierge took our bags from the trunk and carried them a short distance to a waiting jet.

We followed Jane, Frank, and Franny into the cleanest waiting area I think I've ever seen. It smelled like fresh popcorn and fresh-brewed coffee.

"Would you like lunch?" asked the grinning front desk attendant. "We have salmon salad or angus burgers with grilled vegetables. I'm happy to grab you all plates while your luggage is loaded."

I wanted to tell her that she should ask me for my identification. I wanted to take off my shoes and walk through a detector of some kind. I wanted to do what I'd always done when boarding an airplane, but instead, I said, "Not for me, but I'll take the grilled vegetables for Melody."

"Not necessary." Sunny appeared out of nowhere. "I've packed and organized lunches blended from your father's rooftop vegetables. Your mother told me to mix halfways with breast milk and distilled water. Does that sound all right?" I almost looked behind me to make sure she was talking to me. I nodded in response. "May I take her so you can relax on the flight?"

But Melody didn't wait for my answer. She immediately leaned out of my grasp and into Sunny's. Jealousy shot through my chest at the sight of my baby girl smooshing foreheads with this new nanny.

Jane inserted her body between Sunny and me. She smiled widely, holding two boxes—one labeled ANGUS BURGER and the other SALMON SALAD. "Trust me," she said. "You will not want to miss these."

I took them, and the concierge immediately removed them from my hands. "I'll take them to your seat, miss." He bowed to me like I was, well, like I was the daughter of the future VP.

"Right this way," said Jane, bouncing on her Tieks.

"Come on, all of you, Melody first, please. She and Sunny will have a play area in the back of the plane. We're"—she paused to glance at her watch again—"twelve minutes behind now."

I was the last to exit the waiting area and the front desk attendant grabbed ahold of the crook of my elbow. "Enjoy your flight," she said in a whisper. "And your mother is my absolute hero, by the way. But don't tell my husband. He thinks I'm a Republican. Also, sorry for your loss. That must've been horrible."

She released me with a smile, a wink, and a wave.

22

The plane was immaculate, beige leather through and through. The pilots stood at attention as we entered. They treated us like we were somebody. I walked aboard awkwardly, Melody watched cautiously, and my father was unrecognizable.

"Ahoy, Cap'n!" he shouted with a crooked salute. "Proud to make your acquaintances, fellas!"

The pilots' grins sank a bit but they remained polite and turned to take their seats in the cockpit. I thought of Harriet's suggestion that I help my father understand his power. *Talk*, I thought. *Speak*, I thought. *Think*, I thought.

No, *write*.

I took a seat near Melody, just to hear her voice, and found a palm-sized notepad-and-pen combo waiting on the armrest. It was as if the plane knew everything that I needed and was ready to accommodate. I lifted the pad and my hand started shaking a bit.

Write.

Okay.

Write!

Okay.

Write!!!!!!!!!!!!!!!!!!

No.

I placed the pen and pad back on the armrest and slid down in my seat.

No.

Writing made me bleed emotionally, and Jane or Melody or Sunny or Franny and Frank or Dad or Mom didn't need me emotionally raw in this moment. I, instead, needed to be steady and calm for our family's debut.

The engine came alive with a sweet hum and there were no instructions for floatation devices or exits or anything. We backed out of the private tarmac and lifted smoothly into the air like a bird, not a plane. Melody chuckled with Sunny as she watched the blue sky come closer and closer. My father dozed off and I stared at the blank pad that I could no longer fill. Then, I spotted the tip of a scroll in the back pocket of the seat in front of me.

23

Dearest, Scribe,

There is no warranty on a life poorly lived. No money—back guarantee for days not utilized. And believe me, Dearest, youth is a trickster.

Allow me, for your sake and my own, to repeat. <u>Youth is a trickster.</u>

She tricks for so long that you believe she is undying. But her cracks begin to show in aching knees and back. In thinning hair and forgetful brains. In missed moments for which, again, there is no warranty.

I do not think it is fair to sign our names to extend warranties on frivolous things, but not on that which is most precious, our fleeting lives. You, Dear, are but a drop in the bucket. Still, youth is, in fact, a filthy trickster.

Why do I continue to reiterate this to you? Because, I see you. Missing moments. Avoiding them with all your might. Insisting on pushing yourself away from the things that may bring you fun for fun's sake. Punishing yourself. And for what?

This, I fear—the message of this scroll has been vague so allow me to close with directness:

Step off this goddamn aircraft with your head held high! This moment holds the potential to shift the direction of your life. For this moment, there is no warranty. No do-over. No whoopsie daisies. Quit your pouting and enjoy it. And mind your step on those stairs while you're wearing those contraptions on your feet. The world is watching.

Don't let them see you fall, literally or figuratively.

Respectfully,
Your Forescribe

"We touch down in Atlanta in about fifteen minutes," said one of the pilots over the intercom.

I got up to go to the restroom. Instinctively, I ducked at the entrance expecting a typical plane restroom, but this was spacious and spotless with fresh flowers by the sink and a long mirror bordered in tiny lights. I blinked at myself, this time, with Harriet's scroll in mind. *Head held high*, she wrote. *Quit your pouting*, she wrote. *The world*, she wrote, *is watching*.

My makeup, I must admit, was expertly done. Muted, sculpted skin. Lined, lightly shadowed eyes. Well-defined brows with a hint of highlight underneath. Ruby-red matte lip as the focal point. The more I saw it, the more I appreciated it. Liked it? Not quite, but I respected the artistry. The cream suit, also not me, was tailored beautifully. It fit like a suit should, cinched at the waist and just short of the knee. And the necklace, unspeakably perfect. Quiet Storm. Virginia's name for me.

I pulled the gold necklace out of my blouse and gently placed it on top for the world to see. A storm was rising on the inside.

"Everyone please return to your seats and prepare for landing."

I felt the plane shifting lower and lower toward the ground. I went to grab ahold of the door to exit the restroom but stopped myself. I turned back to look myself in the eye and stared for a few seconds.

"Quit your pouting, Ruth." I grabbed the sink, leaned in to the mirror, and whispered to my reflection. "Head up. The world is watching. Do not let them see you fall, literally or figuratively. And . . ."

I snatched the wig from my head.

"You draw the line at wigs."

I lightly wet the ends of my hair and gathered my curls into my signature small puff. If I was going to debut myself to the world, I was not doing so without my natural hair.

The plane's wheels gently touched the tarmac as I reached my seat.

"Madam Vice President!" Jane said with exaggerated air-kisses.

"Maamaaaaaa!" Melody's sweet laugh drowned out all else as she leaped into our mother's toned arms.

"Good job," I whispered for her getting our mother's name on the first try. "Sweet angel."

I stood to meet Mom's gaze. She was a vision in red. She

looked even better than she did on television. But I could see the stress deep in the back of her eyes where no one else, not even my father, knew to look. She was tired to her bones and done with all of this. What I couldn't tell was if she simply needed a long nap or if she'd gotten in over her head.

"Ruth," she said with a respectful smile. "You look just like . . ." She cleared her throat and her nostrils flared a tiny bit. "Well, you look beautiful."

"Velicia," my father said simply.

"Joseph," she replied with a cautious nod.

He cringed in return. He hated his first name. That was his father's name and they'd never gotten along. To call him that was a blunt blow.

"I've gotten word of your behavior." My mother was speaking to him with an authority I both respected and was uncomfortable with. "It is, as you well know, unacceptable."

"You've upended our lives with no notice, Velicia," he spat. "I'd say your selfishness is, as you well know, unacceptable."

The jet's idling engine growled down until you could hear a pin drop.

"Oh no, no, no, no, no, no," Jane interrupted the silence. "This will not do. Not at all. No, no, no."

When she broke through the quiet, everyone began to scatter. The pilots bowed their heads and rushed out of the plane; Franny and Frank followed them but not without tilting their head at my wigless head; and then Sunny squeezed by as well, leaving us alone with only Jane's perfectionist energy.

"This is our—"

"Debut," interrupted my father. "We know."

"Yes," Jane said through bared teeth. "And you could blow this for everyone. Every single voter, desperate to move this country in a different direction. Every donor, some who've given their whole, hard-earned paychecks so that we have a fighting chance at winning this thing. Every family looking for relief under a new administration and you're already bickering? About what? There are people out there starving and here you are in thousand-dollar suits on a private jet."

Jane said it all in one frantic breath. I'd expected her pep talk to be about posture and waving methods, but, in that moment, I realized that she actually believed in the cause. This wasn't just a job to her. This was pure passion and I respected that.

"I'll go first," I said.

Everyone looked at me like I was a Martian.

"Oh, Ruth," my mother replied. "You don't have to—"

"I'll do it," I insisted. "I'll lead and you all follow me down."

Melody smiled and began to bounce in my mother's

arms. My mother's deeply hidden exhaustion was showing just beneath her smile and my father nodded approvingly.

"You should go first," he said to me. "You should."

And so I did.

Before I got a chance to change my mind, I turned to the open breezeway and stood at the top of the red-carpeted stairs where a sea of camera people waited on the tarmac. I did not wave. To wave would not have been me. I stood there, though, taking it all in for a moment, and then, without holding the rails, I made my way down.

Applause and click, click, clicks from cameras. A few people knew to yell my name. "Ruth! Ruth!" I stepped down the stairs, one by one, until, finally, I reached the ground. My mother placed a gentle hand of encouragement on my back, and thankfully, my father smiled beside her. It was an empty smile, but only those closest to him would be able to see that.

"How does it feel to be reunited with your mother?" asked a cameraman.

Another yelled. "You look like royalty, the lot of you."

The next one dared to ask, "Don't you wish Virginia were here?"

"That's enough." Jane's voice pierced the chatter of the camerapeople and she rushed us quickly to the waiting SUV. "Give this family room to breathe. They've had a long flight."

"It's a forty-five-minute flight, Jane," replied one of the cameramen with disappointment in his voice.

"On a fucking private jet, no less." Another cameraman chuckled condescendingly.

"Jesus Christ," said another.

We dipped into the SUV to find more snacks and lunches waiting. "If you're hungry," said the driver before taking off.

"We're going to the Ritz," Jane said while texting voraciously. "Anyone need coffee? We'll need you all on point for Trevor."

"Who the hell is Trevor?" asked my father, and I was glad he did.

"He," Jane said, halting her texting to stare at him directly, "is your much-needed PR coach. He will teach you how not to be a rude mess with zero decorum." She went back to texting. "Publicly, at least."

I noticed my mother staring out the window on her side and holding Melody's hand so tight that it was turning a bit pale. I wanted to ask what was wrong, because something obviously was, but there were six people in the SUV. It was neither the place nor the time to expose her exhaustion. My father was angry with her and he may well have used it against her. Melody was just happy to see her mother outside of a screen. Jane was already about to burst with anxiety. And the driver, for all I knew, could've been supporting the other guy. I kept my mouth shut.

We pulled into the back entrance of the Ritz-Carlton

and we were inundated with gold. Lots of gold, with gold trim on the doors and gold fixtures. As soon as we exited the car, two large men guided us to two waiting elevators. Jane and her team got on one and we four family members got on the other. We were alone as a family for the first time in months.

"You look beautiful, Ruth," my mother said again sadly. "Grown up."

"You really do," added my father. "The wig wasn't you."

"Wait." Mom turned to him, smiling. "They tried to put her in a wig?"

"Ruuuuuuu."

My family was together and laughing on that elevator. It was a glorious ride that should've lasted longer, but Virginia, of course, was missing. The door opened and Jane, Franny, Frank, Sunny, and a man I assume was Trevor stood in the large penthouse.

It was strange to me that as soon as the elevator doors opened, we were in the penthouse. No hallway to walk down. No keycard to insert. No neighbors. An entire floor, open and vast. It, too, was very gold. And more food waited on the buffet table near the conference room.

"Help yourselves to whatever you'd like," said Trevor with a slight English accent. It might have been fake, I couldn't tell. "The strawberries are divine. The thin-cut steak bites are beyond. And the smoked salmon, oh dear Fitzes, you will diiiieee."

What a strange, strange man, I thought. He was large and a bit scraggly, but he moved and spoke like a rail-thin English butler on PBS. His belly hung over his brown belt and he swung it with high esteem as if he'd worked hard for it and was damn well going to show it off. He chef-kissed twice for no reason at all. And he held his glasses so tightly in his huge hands that I was nervous they might crack under the pressure. I liked him.

"Any takers?" he asked, stuffing a thin slice of steak into his mouth. "Your loss. I will insist on coffee all 'round. And Sunny, dear girl, steal away this precious child, if you please."

I watched my mother release Melody to Sunny and I recognized a small, familiar glint of jealousy.

"Everyone gather here, 'round the couches, but don't sit, please. First thing's first, I must evaluate your posture," Trevor said, dipping in and out of his accent. I was no expert, but every few sentences, I heard a hint of unsheddable New Orleans. "Oh, no." He held a wooden ruler to my father's back. "You suffer deeply, dear, from laptop back. Have you seen a chiropractor for this?"

"For my laptop back?" my father replied sarcastically. "It's on my list."

To my surprise, my mother let out a small laugh in response. And to my further surprise, my father laughed with her. They looked like they used to, long ago. Before Virginia . . .

"We'll get one in for you," Trevor said pityingly, and

then placed the ruler against my spine. "I rarely say this, but you have perfect posture, Ruth. Change nothing."

I locked eyes with my mother and she nodded once. Sorrow emitted from her whole body now. It hurt to witness, so I grabbed her hand and led her to an empty bedroom without anyone's approval. She was my mom and I should be able to ask her how she's doing without going through chains of command. I heard objections coming from behind me but ignored them, shutting us alone in a beautiful bedroom with a white leather chaise lounge in the middle and white roses spilling from anything that would stand still.

"You don't look right to me."

In response, she slowly sat on the perfectly made bed and placed her forehead in her hands. I sat next to her. She grabbed her stomach with manicured fingernails and dug in as if trying to peel back skin there. I sensed she wanted to yell out, but refused to.

She opened her mouth and closed it again. And again. She wanted to say something that hurt to say.

"Virginia." I said it for her.

That's when she broke.

What came afterward was not subtle but it was necessary. It was a wailing. I'd never seen anyone do this in real life before. The closest was Meryl Streep in a movie, but even that couldn't touch the anguish I witnessed in my mother. Every moment that passed, she dug deeper into her stomach.

Her meticulous red suit was now wrinkled underneath her hands, bunched and twisted like a used washcloth. Sounds rose from her diaphragm. Low, guttural rasps of real pain.

Jane knocked frantically. "Everything okay in there, ma'am?" Knock, knock, knock, knock, knock, knock, knock, knock . . .

I wanted to scream for Jane to stop, but before I could, my mother crossed the room with one angry stride and flung the door open. Jane stood in the threshold, terrified and shocked. My mother's aura broadcast redder than her suit. She was a tangle of emotion, most of which was now directed at Jane, the messenger. But when my mother spoke, she did so with the rehearsed calm of a Black woman not wanting to be called too angry.

"Jane," my mother began. "I need everyone who's not family to exit the suite. You may come back in an hour's time. No sooner. If you have anything scheduled that is not changeable, respectfully, I don't give a shit. I need this time with my family. Thank you."

My mother gently closed the door and turned to face me. Her plastered-on smile melted and she slid down the door until her butt hit the plush carpet.

"Yes," she said to me, her voice low. "Virginia."

I walked over and joined her on the floor. Shoulder to shoulder, I thought of all those nights on the carpet with Melody. Something about the floor was healing to the

Fitzes. A grounding, I thought. A closeness or a humility or something that stripped away all of the unwanted *extra*. My mother's gorgeous head rested on my shoulder and her long-held tears fell hard.

"I haven't cried once until now," she started. "How could I not cry? I ran. Focused on anything else. Anything." She gulped so loudly that it sounded like a word. "Anything but . . . I ran away."

She went quiet again. She was boxing with herself and losing. Beating herself to a pulp as she likely had every single day since Virginia . . .

What she couldn't know—what she wasn't there to know—was that we all avoided the lowering of that casket in our own ways. Dad traded in his activism and sweater vests for three-piece suits and donuts. Melody stopped sleeping in her crib. And I'd sacrificed my love—words.

"We all ran in different ways," I told her. "Some things are just too hard to stare at without blinking."

Mom lifted her head from my shoulder to stare at me. "I couldn't."

Again, she parted her lips to speak and then glued them shut over and over. Whatever it was she had to say was necessary and hard.

"Couldn't what?" I asked. "Just say it. You need to say it."

There was a pause and I replayed my own words back to myself. *Just say it, Ruth. You need to say it, Ruth.* I was a hypocrite, requesting baring of soul from my mother and holding on to my own like a stubborn child. If I expected transparency, I needed first to give it away.

"I can't go upstairs without breaking," I whispered to her. "She's up there. Hiding in the books and the locked desk and the shelving. She left and somehow floated up there. It feels like she's waiting on something important to happen before she can leave."

I stopped talking to look at my mother. I needed to make sure she wasn't worried I'd lost my mind. And she wasn't. She hung on to every word like I was a preacher and she was a church mother waiting for the Word on Sunday morning.

I continued. *Say her name*, I thought. And do not dare count your words.

"Virginia," I shuddered. "She's up there, and nothing surprises me because of it. Magical things that shouldn't be possible don't shake me. Unexplainable coincidences too unexplainable to actually be coincidences don't give me pause. And you." I turned to her. "Mom. You. I've seen you running. I understand why. Honestly, I don't know if I should envy it or be proud of it or angry at it. Mostly, I just think you're a badass. You left us, yes. That, I cannot sugarcoat. It was wrong, yes. That, I refuse to lie about. But also, Virginia came to this world by way of your body and to watch her being put away, lowered into the ground, the baby you birthed . . . That, I cannot imagine.

"Do not apologize for being human," I told her. "Apologize, instead, for not being honest about being human. Honest." I rested my head on the wall and squeezed my eyes shut. "I've been getting messages from Harriet Jacobs."

I refused to open my eyes.

"I think we've all been getting messages from somewhere," she replied. "I heard the voice of my dead granny on the way to yesterday's congressional hearing. She told me to stand up straight."

"No," I said, eyes still squeezed. "Tangible ones. I can show you if you—"

Knock, knock, knock, knock, knock.

This time, the knocks were timid and terrified rather than frantic, so I assumed they weren't Jane's. I was wrong.

Jane said, "Ma'am, I know it hasn't yet been an hour, it's been, rather, thirteen minutes, but we have a problem."

My mother popped up, back into work mode. Within seconds she had shed all semblance of grief from her fussily dressed body.

24

We hurried to the blaring television in the main room. My mom clutched Melody. Dad watched Mom like she was a live grenade. Go to her, I urged internally. What the hell is wrong with you, man? Go to your wife! But he just kept standing there, scared to face the terrifying emotion of the moment. He had to have heard us in the bedroom, and he chose not to show up. I couldn't help thinking what a missed opportunity that was, and I wondered if he thought the same.

"Where's the remote?" Mom lifted couch cushions and pillows, but it was atop the entertainment console, right where it was supposed to be.

"Here," Dad said timidly.

"Thanks," she replied.

FOX headline: Out-of-touch vice presidential candidate Velicia Fitz claims exhaustion post 45-minute flight on private jet.

MSNBC headline: How long, exactly, is the flight from Birmingham to Atlanta anyway?

CNN headline: Private jets. Are they necessary for what would take 2.5 hours driving?

"What the hell?" asked Mom. "They'll twist anything, won't they?"

"This will pass," Jane said carefully to my mother. "This is a slow news day. News about not much at all. Trevor?"

"I mean"—Trevor shrugged—"environmentalists take this type of thing seriously. And honestly, when I first saw it, I thought it was out of touch, too."

Jane gave Trevor the stank eye for not backing her up.

"What?" he said. "You asked me!"

My mother walked until she and Melody were nose to nose with Trevor. "Well then, how do we fix this?"

"Start by getting your husband to stand up straight."

"Oh, for Christ's sake," Dad said.

"Okay, I'll be the reporter." Trevor walked over to my father and held an invisible microphone to his lips. "Mr. Fitz, Mr. Fitz, Mr. Fitz . . ."

Dad flinched. "Come on, man."

"This is how they will behave," Trevor said, inching

closer into my father's personal space. "This, dears, is the political reporting pool. Trust me when I say it's filled to the brim with sharks."

He'd pronounced it *shawks*. Definitely New Orleans, I thought, and then I wondered why on earth anyone would intentionally hide such a unique, gorgeous accent behind a fake English one.

"Now"—Trevor leaned into my father, dangerously close—"what kind of Democrat takes a forty-five-minute flight on a private jet, sir? You do realize the environmental lobby will have plenty to say about this waste, don't you, sir? Why oh why, sir, aren't you standing up straight? Mr. Fitz, Mr. Fitz, Mr. Fitz . . ."

That's when my father stopped flinching, and to the surprise of all of us grabbed ahold of the invisible mic from Trevor. When he did, Trevor let out a strange gasp like there was actually a microphone to snatch away. I caught myself smiling and then I caught my mother smiling, too. Ah, joy.

Dad began pacing the area as if he owned it. "Mr. Trevor, is that your name, brother?" he asked, but went on without waiting for an answer. "Happy to answer your many questions in reverse numerical order, if you please.

"Let's begin with the latter. Why aren't I standing up straight, you ask? Laptop back, I assume. Too many hours, late ones, after professing my days away about African American history and then running a household. Let me actually amend that answer—laptop slash hard-working father back. It takes its toll.

"Next, do I realize the environmental lobby will express concern? Yes, I understand this and I'm looking forward to speaking with them on how to move forward. Together, we can tackle the climate crisis and I'm eager to learn more about my—and my family's—footprint.

"Finally, what kind of Democrat flies private for a forty-five-minute flight? That, sir, is the wrong question. The correct question, if you please, is what kind of *father* flies private for a forty-five-minute flight? The answer is a terrified one. One who is utterly new to the political scene with two young daughters, one of whom is a *baby*. A father who would utilize every opportunity to keep his daughters safe in the midst of media blitzes and next-level attention we didn't ask for. A father, also, who cannot, *will* not lose another goddamn daughter."

He handed back the invisible microphone and took his seat.

The room stood still.

And then, for a fleeting moment, Mom beamed at my father. Such a small and seemingly insignificant breakthrough, but I saw it. Then, Virginia returned. How long would she haunt this family's potential? She was becoming a wedge between us and good things. A dark cloud blocking out the sun. A dead sister and daughter reopening her casket every second of every day to let us in with her. I hated myself for thinking it and I wondered if anyone else in that room was thinking the same.

Jane shifted and her restlessness spoke volumes. She was such a type A, task-oriented person; I could feel her struggling with the gloominess in the room. She not only wanted to win, but she specifically wanted my mother to win.

Trevor, on the other hand, looked affected. Holding his fake mic to his chest, I swore I saw tears welling up. Franny and Frank turned and began nervously fiddling with their roller racks of clothing.

Then, Mom slowly eased Melody into Sunny's arms and took her seat in front of the television. "I'll call *Lillian Tonight*," she said, choosing work over dealing with the heavy weight of her dead daughter. "She'll surely give me a few moments to clean up this misunderstanding."

Finally, there was Melody.

I watched her intense eyes glowering at our mother. While Melody couldn't yet verbalize her emotions, something strong was happening inside her. Then, as if the crack in the dam finally burst, Melody screamed so loudly that I would've sworn she'd been dropped.

She was still safely in Sunny's arms, but she began kicking and punching so violently that I couldn't believe it was my Melody. One especially hard punch landed on Sunny's eye and she, too, screamed in pain.

I briefly looked to my mother and father, but they were both frozen in place in shock. I grabbed my baby sister underneath her armpits and ran into the bedroom my mother and I had just been in.

Her thrashing continued until we slid onto the floor in front of the bed. Then, her body calmed as she cried. I'd never seen her behave like that. Melody was typically an enviable baby. I'd watched so many kids in her day care act out at drop off and pickup. I'd even witnessed one kid intentionally roll in a muddy puddle on picture day just so her mother wouldn't leave. But Melody? Never. She was every teacher's favorite kid—kind, calm, and easy. But Melody was also introspective. She watched. Waited. Listened and observed. Yes, a baby with depth—but it was the truth. And now, in this pristine hotel room, she was furious that no one was brave enough to address Virginia. And rightly so.

"Can I help?" asked Sunny through a small crack in the door. Her eye was already beginning to shine.

"Thank you," I told her. "But no."

When Sunny left, I eased the door shut with my foot and began humming Pink Floyd's "Wish You Were Here" into Melody's ear until she finally fell asleep in my arms.

I felt myself waiting for a scroll to appear under the door or fly through the window or something. It didn't. It did appear, however, in the innermost pocket of my cream suit jacket.

25

Dearest, oh Dearest,

Never has there been and never will there
be a young woman such as yourself.
Never will there be a moment such as
this.

   It is sad, really, if you take the time
to think of it. And that is, after all,
something I now have in abundance—time.

   I've listened to your song by that
name, if you want to call it that. Time.
It is a yelling more so than a singing, but
I will give you this, the writer, like us, is
a poet.

Ticking away the moments that make up the dull day . . .

Ah, time. Fleeting, manipulative, mind-twisting, back-bending time. Enough of it transforms peaks into valleys. But trees? Time is no match for those.

I adore trees. Have I told you this?

I nearly worship them. They give with no expectation to receive.

I wished trees to shrink down and become my companions. That was a rare thing on the plantation—true friendship. Outside of one's family, I found myself disappointed quite a lot. But time . . .

Alas, time brought about a change.

Ambition is a disease for the young. This is not clear. Ambition is, rather, a disease of those who believe they have an abundance of time. But the older we get, the more it is shed from our bodies like skins from a snake. It doesn't happen all at once, oh no. Selfish ambition falls away and we forget to care about the competition's standing in the race. We then care only for what matters. Ah, pain. Children. Family. The truest of loves.

In my most humble opinion, dear Scribe, the sooner in life you understand this simple fact, the better you will feel at the tail end of it.

There is a debate that crops up every so often and it takes me aback. It is a question of whether time exists at all in the first place. What a stupid proposition. Please excuse my use of the word "stupid" here, dear Scribe, fore I cannot think of a better one.

Of course time exists. Debating the existence of time is akin to debating the existence of gray hairs on the head or clouding of the pupils. It is unwise to take time discussing time. It is, I dare say, a waste of . . . yes . . . time.

This is a rambling letter. The most rambling letter and I will confess why this is the case:

I find myself sitting too long with my thoughts. When I am not writing these scrolls to you, Dearest, I am cursed to sit still and watch.

I watch you and I feel.

I _feel_.

Feeling is a necessary part of being alive, but feeling hurts sometimes. I watch you, Love. Like a mother bird watches her freshly hatched chick. I saw you walking down the stairs of that aircraft. You did it first. You took charge. You will not understand this part at all, because you are not yet a mother. But it hurt watching you try. Even the potential that you might have stumbled hurt. The worry of it hurt. But you did not fall, you triumphed. When you did, I began to worry about the next thing that may or may not happen to you.

I _feel_.

I'd forgotten how much pain it takes to adequately love something. It's debilitating.

For this scroll to be useful to you, I should offer observation and advice. First, let me say that I am so very glad you took that thing off your head. Your hair is more beautiful by a lot.

Secondly, I must apologize for suggesting that you talk to your Father. He is lost.

Thirdly, and this should come as no surprise to you, your Mother is on the verge. She is running too far too fast. A wall is waiting. No Mother—ah, pain—can run that fast without crashing.

Fourth, Melody. She will be the best of us.

And lastly, You. Dearest, You. For the love of all things holy, <u>write something!</u> Write a sentence. Just one. Right now. On the back of this scroll. Do it now. One sentence. There is a pen in the other pocket.

Your Forescribe,
H

As promised, a pink ink pen was in my right jacket pocket. I flipped the scroll over and held the tip of the pen on the parchment until it bled a small pool.

"One sentence," I whispered. "You can write a single sentence."

I used to write compulsively. Uncontrollably, like a doodler doodles. I'd write without thinking of the words first. They'd just flow from mind to fingertips, and now, I couldn't come up with a single sentence. It doesn't have to be profound, Ruth. No one else will read it.

What the hell is wrong with you, write a goddamn sentence!

LIVE! What's the worst that could happen?
LIIIIIIIIWWWWE!!!

I placed the pen back into my jacket pocket and tucked the scroll alongside it. *Live.* There, I'd written. *Live.*

"Bus is here," Jane said, tapping lightly. "Come down when you're ready. We have a bit of time before we need to go. And if you're hungry . . ."

I stopped listening after that. One thing that was abundantly clear, there was no shortage of food on this campaign tour. But my stomach was too unsettled to eat anything. Melody began to stir and she woke up smiling.

"Hey there," I said to her sparkling eyes.

"Ruuuuu!"

26

Stepping aboard the campaign-tour bus, the first thing that caught my attention was new-car-smell times a million—leather on leather on leather on beige, opulent leather. My eyes were overwhelmed trying to decide what to focus on. Warm tea lights glowed along the ceiling, but I couldn't find the source of them. They just sort of appeared out of nowhere like stars in the night. The thick-planked hardwood reflected the glow, illuminating a path toward the fireplace. Yes, a flickering fireplace on a bus.

I waved my hand in front of the fire but it wasn't giving off any heat. It was there for weird decoration in eighty-degree Atlanta. Overhead was an unreasonably large television framed like a painting, and beside it there was a spotlighted bar fully equipped with brown and clear liquor and a wide selection of beer.

Melody began to wiggle her way down and she went straight for a small fridge to find more snacks. I bent down next to her to face a hodgepodge of rich people's food. On the top row were drinks organized from shortest to tallest like soldiers in a line. Underneath the soldiers was a large, square platter filled with such strange foods, all of which were labeled with tiny pink flags: caviar, truffles, brie with pâté and toast. On the bottom shelf was a whole cooked smiling lobster with a fanned-out lemon on its head like a crown.

I closed the refrigerator and sighed. Who did these people think we were? I mean, I had nothing against rich people but pâté?

That's when Jane stepped onto the bus, followed by her crew and then Dad, and finally, Mom, who was on the phone trying to clean up the lingering flight mess.

"Oh no," she said, her smile strained. "No more private jets. Now, we're on a ratty old bus. We're regular folks, just like you. I was born and raised in Birmingham, a few blocks up the road from Dynamite Hill. I remember my father standing on the doorstep late at night, shotgun in hand, protecting our small home from the worst of the world. I'm a red-blooded American, Diane, just like you. You and me, actually, we have quite a bit in common. We should grab coffee sometime. When this whole campaign has come to a close."

There was a pause and I assumed Diane was responding in my mother's ear. As my mother fake-laughed at whatever Diane had said, I looked around the ratty bus. It could easily cost over a million dollars. I felt weird even being on it, let alone pretending it was ratty.

"She's getting a little too good, huh?" Dad sat next to me.

I was surprised because he hadn't been that close in days. He was embarrassed, I think, and he should've been. But what he had said about Virginia into that invisible microphone was real. He'd said he couldn't lose another daughter, but what he hadn't said was he was slowly losing his wife as well. As he watched her I realized his laptop back had nothing to do with posture. He was carrying grief in his shoulders. He missed my mother. Just like Melody did, and me too.

"Are you proud of her?" I asked him.

He looked taken aback by the question. "What do you mean?"

I stayed quiet and gave him an opportunity to think. It was a large question, even though it was just five words. If he was truthful, the answer would be loaded with so many things—jealousy, anger, bewilderment, shock, awe, and so on. As he contemplated the answer, I thought about the difference between pride and proud.

Pride was what I'd seen in my father over the past few days. The wicked pride of a man too proud to genuinely be proud of a woman outdoing him. Then, I thought of the act of actually being proud of someone else—a satisfaction, an honor to know that a human being is finally receiving her hard-fought appreciation. Pride versus proud. Times like these I stood in absolute awe of the English language. It was a beautiful thing of frustration and confusion.

And it had my utmost respect.

"Pride comes before a fall," he replied, but didn't elaborate.

"Oh yes, Diane," Mom said into the phone. "When we win this thing, we'll talk about you getting those coveted press pool credentials. But we have to win first, right? So this flight nonsense needs to be pushed out of the news cycle. And quick. We don't want a deplorables moment, now do we? All right, then. Thanks for the call. Talk soon. All right. Ha ha ha. Yes, then. Okay, then. All right, bye-bye." She hung up and said, "Dear God, that woman hates to stop talking."

"Ma'am?" Jane asked, still cautious. "We can't promise everyone credentials."

"Well, I know that, Jane," she replied, as if there was nothing wrong with empty promises. "I need Melody. Now."

She proceeded to unbutton her suit and remove her breast. Melody toddled down the plush aisle of the bus and fell naturally into Mom's chest. I hadn't seen Melody nurse directly from my mother in so long and I wasn't sure if she'd remember how, but she did. As if no time had passed at all, they fell into a quiet zen that made me remember Virginia. And I was becoming sick and tired of remembering Virginia. The longing to forget her was followed by the urge to count my words.

In the distance, I heard someone singing badly. And then Judy Harrison, daughter of the presidential nominee, appeared in the doorway of the bus, earbuds in, head bobbing, and shamelessly belting show tunes.

"Suddenly, Seymour! He purified meeeeee!"

"Oh no," said Frank. "Here she comes."

"Oh no," echoed Franny.

"Oh no," Jane finally added. "Guard your ears."

"Hello, dream guys and dolls!" Judy sang out with arms wide open. "I'm happy to introduce myself. I! Am! Juddddyyy!"

She held her *y* longer than any human lungs ever should. As she did, her wiggly spirit fingers bent back and forth in weird ways and her legs flapped together until I heard her inner thighs slap against each other.

"Jane! Oh, hi there, Jane. Glad to see you. Franny, Frank, pleasure, pleasure! Madam Future Vice President." She bowed dramatically. "It is always such a joy to be in your presence. I assume this is your precious daughter."

Melody peeked up from my mother's breast but refused to release it. I heard her familiar coo, the one she only gave to her immediate family. *Good sign*, I thought. Melody identified decent people immediately with that special sound.

"Mr. Fitz!" Judy said, bouncing a few steps toward my father with pointed toes. "I've heard of your incredible work in the space of history and I am in absolute awe, dear sir."

My father liked her immediately, too. "Why," he said with his palm on his chest, "I don't know what to say. Thank you, young lady."

And then she turned her attention to me, but she didn't say anything. Instead, she turned to Jane. "How long before we have to leave?"

Jane, annoyed, glanced at her watch. "Seventeen minutes."

Judy grabbed my hand and said, "Seventeen minutes, perfect. Let's go!"

Jane stood to object but Judy began singing loudly to drown out her objections.

"Judy," my mother said with the unruffled depth of an authoritarian. "You two can't just prance around the city anymore. You'll be recognized."

Judy turned on her heel to slow-move to my mother like a mosquito to a blue porch lamp. It was an immediate change of demeanor, as if my mother's voice had extracted the manic show tunes and inserted obedient calm.

My mother had something both scary and amazing. Something I hadn't noticed until that moment—real power. She wielded it effortlessly. I squinted at her, trying to figure out if even she understood it or not. This was the opposite of what most people thought to be power; this outma-neuvered the Mercedes/house-on-the-hill foolishness that most men sought. This, I realized, was the kind that could win this election by a landslide.

In a low, sweet voice, and with the eyes of a baby basset hound, Judy said, "Please."

I couldn't tell if Judy was acting. If I had to guess, I'd think she was not. No one could look that pitiful on pur-pose. They stared at each other in a silent standoff, then Judy continued.

"We just need to breathe, Ruth and me. Don't you ever need to breathe, ma'am?"

I smiled a bit watching them. They both had power. My mother's was obvious, but Judy's was hidden underneath her exaggerations.

"And let the Secret Service stay close," my mother said. I saw my father try to stand in protest but my mother shot him a look.

"Thank you, ma'am!" Judy exclaimed, hyperactive energy returned.

And just like that, we were off the bus and walking the sidewalks of downtown Atlanta with two very large men on our tails.

27

"I love Atlanta," Judy said in singsong. "Don't you?"

I hadn't so much as looked around since we'd been there. But when Judy asked the question, I opened my eyes. There were people coming and going in every direction. In and out of the large stone library and cafés and gift shops. There were so many skinny buildings that held art galleries selling original paintings. I wondered how they all survived so close to one another. Wouldn't they choke one another out, like a row of Starbucks? But the answer seemed to be no.

I finally nodded in response.

"It really is a wonderful place!" she replied to my silent nod. "East Court is this way! Let's see how far we are from my favorite bookstore."

Although we'd just met, Judy grabbed my hand again

and pulled me across the street. Her palm was clammy but I didn't mind. She was a girl who was the opposite of me, and I, like Melody, wanted to coo at her.

She was so alive and present. She seemed to treat Jane's seventeen minutes like treasures, leaping through them, whereas I would've just sat still in those minutes, saying to myself seventeen minutes wouldn't be long enough to do anything at all. But there we were, standing in front of the sweetest little bookstore—Little Shop of Stories.

The place was overflowing with teenagers anxiously awaiting a visit from a local author. They were giddy with anticipation and that made me happy.

"Look!" Judy exclaimed. "It's Gardenia Murphy!"

I let out a small gasp. Gardenia Murphy had written the first three books in a seven-part Black sci-fi fantasy series called Blessers and Cursers. I, like everyone else, was obsessed with the series and wanted desperately to meet Ms. Murphy myself, maybe even grab a signed copy of . . .

"Oh my God," I said with my hand over my mouth. "What day is it?"

"It's Wednesday."

"Oh my God! Her fourth book came out yesterday!" Uncharacteristically, I ran up to a total stranger and asked, "Is this her official launch? What is this? What is this?"

Instead of answering, the equally excited girl about my age reached into her Little Shop of Stories tote bag and lifted out the brand-new, Bible-thick copy of the fourth installment of Blessers and Cursers called *Who Let the Light In*.

I nearly passed out. "We have to get it!" I turned back to Judy, who was mischievously glancing at her phone.

"Jane's sent twelve texts," she said, grinning. "So far."

"How long has it been?"

"Eighteen minutes exactly," Judy replied. "This line will take, say, an hour. Easy. I'm down to wait if you are."

I thought of it. Then, I shook my head. "It's irresponsible. There's no way. We just wasted another minute standing here. It'll take at least six to get back to the bus. Nine if we run into too many red lights. Come on. No. We can't. No."

I'd said so many unnecessary words that I wanted to wash my mouth out. I hadn't done that for a long, long time. As we began walking, I wondered what Harriet Jacobs would think. Two dead people—Virginia and Harriet—dictating my thoughts more than anyone with breath in their lungs, even me.

"Stop," I said to Judy, who perked at the word. "What are the odds? On our little seventeen-minute walk around a random corner, we just mosey up to the launch of the latest book by Gardenia Murphy. Judy," I said, grabbing her by the shoulders and staring directly into her amber-hued eyes. "We will get in monumental trouble. Do you realize that?"

She eagerly nodded in response.

"Jane won't like it," I said as she added a smile to her nod.

"Your dad won't, either," I told her, and she threw in a shimmy. "All of them. But Judy, what are the odds? This is our shot to meet one of the best writers living."

And that's when Judy couldn't hold on to it anymore. She nearly burst into the air, yelling, "We are not throwing away our shot! We are not throwing away our shot! We are not throwing away our . . ."

I grasped her hand this time. "Come on!" I snuck a peek at the two Secret Service guys across the street talking into their wrists. "We'll have to lose them."

We ducked to the back of the line, which snaked around quite a few storefronts. Peering through people's elbows and knees, I saw the Secret Service scrambling to find us. They jogged here and there until finally deciding to go north.

Waiting in line with any other person I'd just met would've been excruciating, even if it was for the new Blessers and Cursers. But not with Judy. She seemed genuinely present and curious and mischievous in ways that I desperately wanted to be deep down on the inside. I thought of her trending hashtag on Twitter—#loonyjudy.

I recalled hundreds of thousands of people tweeting that. And though I rarely ventured anywhere near social media, I remember having a small chuckle at it myself. It felt innocent at the time, because she wasn't real. She was a wealthy, spoiled politician's daughter with caviar trays in the minifridge. What's a harmless chuckle at a harmless hashtag?

But now, of course, here she was. Bouncing and twirling

and whisking me around a city I would never have explored without her. She was not Loony Judy at all—she was more herself than anyone I'd ever met.

"Magnets!" she yelled out. "We have to start a tradition, right here right now, everywhere we go, we get two magnets. One for me, one for you. But! We have to come up with four facts about the magnets and we cannot leave whatever town we're in until we find the ones with those specifications. Make sense?"

I tilted my head.

"It'll all come together," she said. "I'll decide on the first of the four. Okay, all magnets must be the cheapest ones in the store. No matter how crappy they look, we have to choose the cheapest. Now you, second fact."

"Uh," I said. "Hmmm." I was already overthinking this. "Uh, they have to have the color orange in them?"

"Oh, oh, oh!" She exclaimed, obviously encouraging me along. "That's a good one! Cheapest and orange, that'll be a helluva goose chase, I love it. Number three, I know! We have to haggle when we buy them."

I laughed because I was horrible at haggling. "Okay, last of the four, we have to write about the moment," I said. "At least a sentence about the circumstances in which we bought them. Is that a good one?"

She beamed. "That's perfect."

I beamed back at her. That would be my way of forcing a pen in my hand to paper. Now, I had no choice. I'd be writing again, even about something small and insignificant like magnets and where they came from. Harriet would be so proud.

"Can you hold our place in line while we run into this store to grab magnets?" Judy asked an annoyed-looking lady behind us who I certainly wouldn't have trusted to hold our place in line. She reluctantly nodded or shrugged, I couldn't tell which.

"Thanks!" Judy replied. "There are some over here, next to the sunglasses."

Judy released my hand and ran toward the tower of magnets. She spun it around and around so fast that I thought it might separate from its base. More than a few were shaped like flip-flops with ATLANTA written on them, and I wondered what a flip-flop had to do with Atlanta. Then there was fruit. Every type you could think of—banana, watermelon, grapes, apples, lemons. The fruit made me think of my dead grandmother's refrigerator. When we were little, Virginia and I would spend hours arranging and rearranging the fruit into new shapes and sometimes curse words. Then, quotes. Albert Einstein quotes, Michelle Obama quotes, even one from Radiohead that read WHEN I AM KING YOU WILL BE 1ST AGAINST THE WALL. Harsh.

My favorite ones were the cityscapes. They varied depending on point of view. Some showed Atlanta as a lively city, bright and breathing. In others, it was a calm place with horse-drawn carriages in the moonlight. The rest were random—a Georgia peach here, a license plate there, even an aquarium turtle or two.

"Kind sir?" Judy called out to the grumpy-looking clerk. "Which magnet is the cheapest?"

He motioned us to the back of the store and said, "Clearance."

On the way to the clearance section, we passed snacks and tampons and oil for the engine and air fresheners and condoms and very old bananas. It felt like a small journey to get to that clearance section, and when we did, I was not disappointed to find the weirdest collection of magnets.

There were only three to choose from. The first was an old dusty Coke bottle with real liquid inside that I assume at one time was brown. It had been sitting so long that it faded to a green puke color. The second, another peach, but the stem was missing and it looked more like a well-toned butt. And the third, ah yes, the third was of the 1996 Atlanta Olympics. The orange flame twisting up like an ice cream cone and it, too, was faded so badly I thought it might be vintage.

"I can't believe no one has bought this," said Judy before picking it up. "Could be worth something. How much, kind sir?"

"Arghh," he replied as he rounded the counter to join us at clearance. "Two dollars."

"One." I forced myself to say it out loud.

"Arghh," he again replied. "One, okay, one."

"We'll take the butt, too," Judy added. "Two bucks for both, final offer."

"Arghh," he said with a small smile. "Come on, then."

We bought them and two small writing pads, and refused the bag. I slipped my Olympics in my pocket and Judy placed her butt in hers.

"We'll write on the buses, deal?" she asked, glowing.

"Deal," I replied, believing at that moment I was glowing, too.

28

The line had moved quite a bit.

"How long were we in there?" I asked.

Judy looked at her phone. "Long enough for Jane to send sixteen more text messages."

As soon as Judy said Jane's name, I saw her standing across the street staring straight at us like we were mischievous three-year-olds in enormous trouble. Completely ignoring the traffic, she bolted across the street and my heart leaped in my chest because I thought she might be hit by a car. Thankfully, she was not hit. I didn't envy the driver who'd dare take on Jane.

"Oh!" Judy exclaimed as Jane reached us. "How on earth did you find us?"

"How did I . . ." Judy couldn't get the words through her

flabbergasted lips. Instead, she held her phone in the air and showed us ourselves trending on Twitter.

Twitter.

The place where I found out that my sister had died.

Twitter.

The hell site that dropped the most devastating news of my life on my then-whole family.

Twitter.

I hated that little blue bird. I wanted to choke it out and let it die. But there it was, tweeting away. Alive and well, excitedly creating a ridiculous narrative about Judy and me.

The first thing I saw was the hashtag (#loonyjudy). I hated it now. It was not funny. Not in the least. Actually, it was downright mean and made me want to throw Jane's phone at the lady who had no intention of holding our place in line.

Then, I saw the name they'd given to me—#unrulyruthy. I laughed because, how?

"How am I—" I started to ask Jane, but she interrupted.

"This is how!"

She pressed play on a video of me leaping into the air about the newest Blessers and Cursers book launch. They'd transformed my rare display of genuine excitement into a viral meme that made me look like I was unhinged.

"Let's go before you do more damage here," whispered

Jane, waving the bus toward us. "And for goodness' sake, wave."

I looked around to see that everyone in line was now watching us; even Gardenia Murphy's phone camera was recording our every move. I waved nervously at Gardenia, who'd abandoned her own signing line to jog in our direction.

My stomach hurdled in my gut as I watched her braid-out bouncing in the breeze. She was taller than I thought she'd be, around five foot nine. She wore an ankle-length splashy maxi dress that picked up every bit of the windy day. Beautiful. She'd recently made the tabloids, rumored to be dating a famous rapper. And last month, *People* magazine had listed her as one of the most beautiful people alive, which was rare for an author. I'd read her reaction when she'd been chosen. She'd simply said, "Holding on to beauty is like holding water in one's palms. While I still have a few drops in my hands, you've given me this honor and I thank you. I do, however, hope you value the endless, boundless, bottomless beauty of my words until eternity." And yes, with pride, I memorized her words.

"Hey," she said to me as if she weren't legend.

"Hey," I said back to her as if I weren't ready to faint.

"Can I get a quick selfie before you go?" she asked me. Me!

"Uh," I replied, and the crowd began to clap.

I turned to see that the bus had pulled up and my mother had stepped out. She was a bright red spot underneath an invisible spotlight walking toward us. Jane forced a smile.

"How's everybody doing?" Mom yelled. Her voice was beginning to suffer under all of the yelling. "Beautiful here in Atlanta, idnit?"

The crowd responded as if the Beatles had shown up.

She closed in on us. "Gardenia Murphy, the one and only," said my mother, and I was surprised she knew who Gardenia Murphy even was. "Pleasure to meet you."

"Ma'am," Gardenia replied. "The pleasure is mine."

"Would you like a . . ." my mother asked, motioning to Gardenia's phone.

"Oh, yes, ma'am! I'd be honored."

"Let's see," Mom said, looking around for the best backdrop. "You know what? Let's do one with your fantastic crowd in the background! How y'all feel about that?"

The crowd jumped up and down. I watched for someone to step out of line but every single person was excited. Even the grumpy clerk and the lady who wouldn't hold our space smiled widely for the photograph. Were there seriously no Republicans in Gardenia Murphy's line, I wondered. I glanced over at my mother, and, for the first time, thought she had a real chance at becoming the vice president of the United States. She was undoubtedly a superstar. Even Gardenia Murphy's bright light dimmed in her presence.

"Say it with me, crowd!" Mom yelled, handing Gardenia's phone to unhappy Jane. "One! Two! Three! Cheeeeese!"

And just as quickly, Mom waved goodbye to everyone and placed a firm hand on my lower back. I knew exactly what that meant from all those lengthy church services as a child. That hand meant let's get the hell out of here before we get caught up in an hour-long prayer circle of church ladies.

We stepped onto the bus and my mom collapsed into her seat. "I need a nap and some ginger tea," she said, almost to herself, but Jane quickly got busy letting down the back-most couch into a queen-sized bed and boiling a kettle for tea in the bus's mini-kitchen.

I watched Jane press hidden buttons in the luxury bus. One of those buttons revealed a pocket door to create total privacy for the queen bed in the back of the bus. Another button made a reading shelf pop out and Jane placed an iPad on it along with the piping-hot mug of ginger tea. The final button she pressed let down a small television with headphones attached for personal viewing.

"Please tell me this isn't more briefing material," said my mom as she made her way to the comfortable-looking setup. "What now?"

"Another conflict brewing in one of the insecure regions," Jane said cryptically. "You'll see in the videos and notes. Definitely something they'll ask about in debate. Spend, I'd say, about three hours studying that and then you can rest up for the next stop."

"And what's the next stop?" Mom asked.

"Memphis," she replied. "Fundraiser."

My mother's tired head fell back onto the headboard and her eyes wandered over to my dad, longing for his help.

In the chaos of Gardenia and Jane and Judy and Mom and the crowd and Twitter and everything, I'd forgotten he was there. I felt horrible about that. He looked from my mother to me and got up to join her on the bed. Then, they closed the pocket door, disappearing behind it. I caught myself silently praying that they got along, at least tonight.

Then, I looked around for Judy but she wasn't there.

"Judy's on the other bus," Jane replied to my thoughts. "Thank God, let's get out of Atlanta before traffic hits."

The driver began rolling slowly and stopped abruptly at a chaotic knock on the door. I smiled, assuming it was Judy, but it was Gardenia, holding an armful of signed copies of *Who Let the Light In.*

"Forgot to drop these off to you guys," she said, seemingly in awe of the bus or maybe us, I couldn't tell which. "Wow."

And she stepped down, back into Atlanta.

"For goodness' sake," Jane said, exasperated. "Let's go."

29

Harriet's letter fell out of the topmost copy of *Who Let the Light In*.

Dearest, Scribe:

To read is to go. To read is to sink into something larger and more powerful than only yourself. To read, ah, to read, is second only to . . . To write.

So, Dearest, go read.

Your Forescribe,
H

30

It was the shortest scroll yet. I couldn't tell if that was a good thing or a bad one, but I wanted more from her. I longed for her wisdom. Her direction. Her power. I was coming to rely on Harriet's scrolls. They were drawing me out into the daylight. I reread her short letter and folded it to create a bookmark for *Who Let the Light In*.

Jane popped up.

"Fine!" she hollered into her phone as she walked toward me. "Judy says she needs to speak to you and it's an emergency. Why on earth don't you have a phone with you, anyway? Frank? Please have a phone waiting for this child in Memphis."

I held the phone to my ear and didn't get to say hello before Judy started talking. "Have you read the first chapter?" she said so quickly I couldn't answer. "I cannot believe the Blessers and the Cursers are actually related to one another! It's madness! Gardenia Murphy is a genius! She's built a whole world in three books and now, in the fourth, torn the whole thing down! It's savage! And Little is actually a—"

"Stop! Stop! Please don't tell me any more until I catch up with you," I said, holding the phone away from my ear to make sure she didn't let anything else slip. "I'll start now."

"K-bye!"

"Bye."

I handed the phone back to annoyed Jane and opened the book to see if it'd been inscribed to me. It read:

Ruth,

Thank you for reading. Thank you for supporting local book-stores.

Gardenia (and she'd drawn a tiny gardenia over the *i* in her first name)

I knew that the inscription was likely pre-written and she'd simply added my name atop but still, it felt amazing. I opened it to Chapter 1 and quickly lost myself in a world so intricately woven by another master Scribe.

31

Memphis was sleeping when we arrived and so was everyone on the bus. Jane, too, phone grasped firmly in hand, had finally dozed off. I'd made it to Chapter 12 of Gardenia's novel without breathing. This book had already been a wild ride and I had zero plans of sleeping until it was finished. Besides, I couldn't risk anyone blabbing the ending before I had a chance to know for myself.

Snaking our way into the city center, a small but active nightlife came into view. Beale Street. But we quickly rolled past all of that and into an enormous cordoned-off area on the street in front of the Peabody Hotel.

"Jane," the bus driver hissed, and I realized I still didn't know his name.

Jane popped up as if she hadn't been in a deep sleep and flitted off the bus in a blink. I saw her determined head bobbing toward the front desk, where she picked up a few frilly gift bags. The attendant craned her neck around Jane to catch a glimpse of the bus and I slumped in my seat, though, of course, the windows were dark. I wanted to put myself on do not disturb and read for as many hours as it took.

Jane came back on the bus and walked straight to me, holding out one of the three gift bags.

"Cell phone," she said. "Already programmed and set up. You don't have to do anything except keep the thing with you and reply when you're texted. Our calendars are synced; that way, you'll know what time you need to be where and which city we're headed to next. Appearances, too, are already entered along with day-before alerts and trainings. Tomorrow, you and Judy will be spending a much-needed day with Trevor to work on . . . presentation. Also in the bag, you'll find articles on past first daughters, the good, the bad, and the downright unruly." Jane caught herself and locked eyes with me.

"That hashtag is ridiculous, by the way," she said with actual sympathy in her gaze. "You're the least unruly child of a politician I've ever worked with." She started to walk away. "Oh, and throwing that thousand-dollar wig away without asking was costly, but you look much more beautiful without it. It was the right thing. But next time, just give it back, deal?"

I nodded to her.

"Deal," she stated before flicking on the bus's lights. "Everybody up and out. Presidential floor awaits."

32

I woke with the nearly finished book on my chest and a scroll tucked neatly in my hand.

Dear, Scribe:

I apologize for my short letter prior. The reason? I recall being lost in the all—consuming adventure of books and I wanted you to dive deep into the unique intricacies of words. I do hope, dear Scribe, that an itch comes over your fingers to write yourself, but alas.

I have a small story to tell in this letter. Small, actually, this story is not.

So, I have a story to tell. That is what I should've said.

The human spirit is as fragile as a fallen feather, even a drip drop of rain can ruin it.

I've seen countless spirits ripped and broken apart for sport. Then, along comes a Scribe of the time. We are a rarity. Usually quiet and unassuming. Sometimes we vanish into the tapestries until we're so invisible that people speak freely as if we aren't even there. Sometimes we lose our words to the harshness of life. And sometimes, Dearest, we allow the ghosts to take control.

I once wrote, "There is something akin to freedom in having a lover who has no control over you."

I think of that quote often. It was written through beautiful, albeit complicated, emotion and trauma. A reaching out for freedom without seeing any real way to touch it. A longing for love in some form. Any form. A near desperation to escape the underneath of someone else's foot.

Control, ah yes, there you are. Pain. Anger. Rage.

Control is the drug of choice for the sadistic. It is also an attempt to fill an empty soul. One who wishes to control another human being deserves no place in the world, in my humble opinion.

My instinct is to crumple this scroll and begin again, I'll admit. I'm diving deep into a blackened space in my heart. Fore, Dearest, I am still angry.

I set out, in this letter, to share with you a story and now I struggle to recall which. I only now am drowning in the rage of the formerly caged. It is all-consuming and with all of my heart I pray you never understand it.

One who seeks to take control of another seeks to kill them on the inside. These are the bastards that laugh at funerals. These are the ones who made me question why the world existed at all. Why, God, won't you simply snip them from the face of the earth? Clip them like the rife weeds choking color from the flourishing garden. But then, I say, along comes a Scribe to do the necessary snipping themselves.

Alas, Dearest, nothing is more dangerous to one who seeks to control a narrative than a writer with a pen in her hand.

I know this may seem foreign to you. Again, I am wading in my own emotions at the moment, and for that, with the utmost sincerity, I apologize. I do have a point to make. And I am again having the urge to rip this scroll to bits and start again fresh but I have more respect for you, Scribe, than to waste the words above, however rambling they may be. I write them now through the welling of tears. I fear reading them back, fore they may cause the dam to break apart. I will keep them raw and move along to the most important subject—you.

You are not controlled, like I was, by the wicked men. You are, however, controlled by ghosts.

I fear I cannot tell you now which is worse. I do not have the foresight nor hindsight to know, but instinct says that your haunting may be of the all-consuming sort. The ghost of glorious Virginia.

I've never mentioned her in any of my letters. I've been anxious to do so, I'll admit. She is a spot so soft that I fear her name written may take away more of your precious words. I write her name now, because I sense in you a shift.

Emotion, again, in my humble opinion if you please, is, or rather should be, one of humanity's most treasured gifts. Emotion adds interesting flavor to an otherwise bland landscape. Think of it, Dearest, how boring life would be without tears and laughter and love and rage. How mundane.

But the stupidest, and loudest, among us shun the powerful possession of emotion. They suggest we stiffen our upper lips when we want to scream out. They call us emotional beings as if that's an insult. They misunderstand loudly and convince others that emotion is weakness when, in actuality, it is our greatest strength.

The shift in you, dear Scribe, that I've sensed is of the emotional persuasion. And it surrounds your ghost, Virginia.

I feel your longing for your sister transforming into resentment. I suspect your sadness is changing to anger. I sense no longer a sadness at the mention of her name, but now, offense.

I do not judge this sentiment. I want to tear this letter, at least in half, because I fear it may come off as judgmental. No. I judge not. I see myself in you. My rage holds me as tightly as it ever has, hundreds of years after the death of my evildoers. That, Dearest, is what happens when you fail to adequately address that which seeks to control you.

There is no such thing as letting it be. No sleeping off that which has you by the throat. You must stare hard at that thing in its eyes for it to retreat.

Or, I dare say, write it!

Ah. Before I end this letter that I want so badly to burn to floating specks, I will after all tell you that story:

There was a girl once who wrote with the heart of a bird. Flying high and pumping blood through her tiny body until she was high enough to kiss the sky with her perfectly pointed beak. But the delicate tip of her beak got stuck in the sun. She pulled and pulled with all of her precious energy. She flapped her bright wings until she was too tired to flap anymore. Then, exhausted and ready to die, she stopped her flapping and was still.

She lifted her chin and stared directly at the molten, angry, raging sun in its vicious face. The sun let off a few threatening puffs of orange death but she could not be moved from her frozen stare.

The sun flinched.

Not her, Dearest, the sun.

She took on the angriest beast and only then realized it was only a child's drawing of the sun. A paper cutout. Her heart was always more powerful than that sun she'd feared. And all she needed to do all along to conquer it was to stand still in front of it, and give it a hard honest stare. Only then did it fall to her feet where it belonged.

Face your ghosts, Precious Heart. Do it. Or, yes. Dare I do say, _write it!_

> Your elaborately
> rambling and
> sometimes completely
> incoherent Forescribe,
> Harriet

33

I didn't give myself time to reflect on the letter. Instead, I placed the magnet on the plush bedspread and took out the notepad that Judy and I had bought in Atlanta. I began, dear God, to write.

Dear Forescribe:

I don't know how to do any of this. I haven't put pen to blank paper in a long time. You know that. I exist mostly inside of my head now. Writing to you feels a bit like writing to the ghost you mentioned in the previous scroll.

I have a few questions for you, if that's all right.

1) Are you real? I guess a follow-up to that question is am I losing my mind?
2) Have you met Virginia? I guess a follow-up to that is did she send you to me?
3) Why me?

I'll make that the final question even though I have so many more. But I have to elaborate on that one, if that's okay.

I'm nobody.

I'm not writing that to fish for compliments, either. I'm literally nobody. I think that's why I'm having trouble fully embracing that I haven't simply lost my mind and am imagining your existence.

You're Harriet Jacobs.

Your novel should be required reading for every human being walking the earth. Your strength to survive what you've already shared with me is unbelievable. And yet, you chose me? I can't understand it.

All of these things are happening to me now. I've gone from a silent Birmingham brownstone to a private jet to a plush bus to presidential suites in less than a week. But most of all, you.

You have to understand how improbable you actually are. No offense, but you're dead. I think? Maybe that should be question number four.

4) Are you dead?

If the answer is yes, Harriet (is it all right that I call you Harriet?), I must be spiraling mentally somehow. If the answer is no, I don't understand.
I'm sorry, I have another question.

5) What do you want me to do, exactly?

You seem to want me to release my ghosts, help my dad be a better person, live life to the fullest, forgive my mom for something I have no control over, and most of all, write.
Again, no offense, but I'm sixteen years old. This all feels enormous. Everything feels too large and out of reach.
I can't help but think of your beautiful story about the bird's beak stuck in the sun. Am I that bird? Or are you that bird? Or are we both that bird together?
Maybe I'm stuck on one side of the sun and you're stuck on the other.
You are a writer. You are a Scribe. I cannot claim the title, it is, yes, too large for me. But for the sake of the story, we both write our moments, yes? You write yours on the side of the sun where you now know the sun is a ruse. A paper-thin beast

that could never have burned you in the first place. But I still cower on the other side.

I look around and see myself becoming something different and I cannot lift my beak to its intimidating face. I, instead, shield my eyes to its brightness. It's largeness.

I fear that I am not worthy.

That's maybe my final question:

6) How am I possibly worthy?

One more...

7) Will I ever not fear the sun?

> I cannot sign this as your scribe, I do not feel enough,
> Ruth

Someone had left a tray of food at my bedside and a perfectly folded pair of gray pajamas sat in the chair in the corner. I wanted to shower the travel off me, but I couldn't move. I was stuck in the heavy place of having written.

After going so very long without writing, it felt like I'd tapped a drip drain directly to my soul and diminished myself. I needed to disappear.

I fingered through the remaining pages of *Who Let the Light In* to see that I'd saved about twenty pages plus acknowledgments. I dove in to get rid of myself for a few moments.

34

I couldn't tell if I was crying because the book was over or if I was crying because the book was sad. That's the true sign of a master scribe, I think. To leave the reader in a state of emotional longing is part of the craft. And I was there.

I began stuffing my mouth with flagged foods that I'd never tasted. Only then did I realize how long it'd been since I'd eaten anything sustaining. When the tray was empty, again I sat in silence. I ripped out Harriet's letter, picked up the pen, and turned to a blank sheet of paper.

Dear Dad:

I am disappointed in you. This is a hard thing to write because I believe—no, I know—it will hurt you. But lately, pain has been our common denominator. Shared pain and heavy silences. I love you. I'm proud to be your daughter. I believe in you. I always have done. But I am also, simultaneously, disappointed in you.

No one can attain perfection. No one can win all the time. No one deserves to be looked up to from the day they're born until the day they die. You have had that unattainable expectation right up until your wife (my mother) eclipsed you.

That, too, is hard to write. Because I have zero doubt in my mind or heart that it will crush you to read this from your own silent child. Still, it's the truth. Mom is not Birmingham famous like you were. She is global and you, Dad, are going to have to accept that or you will lose yourself in regret and ugliness.

Jealousy is ugly. And you've been dipped in it. Rid yourself of that and you'll see that you have an opportunity to show men how to support shining wives. It's a good look. I swear to you. That will be something worth being remembered for. But grimacing in the background as your spouse holds the room is just plain ugly.

And Virginia.

I don't know the right way to say this. This is part of the reason I've limited my words. I do not know what to say while walking through the nightmare of Virginia's death. It really is, isn't it? A communal nightmare. The worst part is we aren't sharing it. You, me, Mom, Melody, we've created bubbles to protect ourselves from one another's grief, but the solitary kind we've chosen might be worse.

What I do not want to write is that Virginia is at the root of our nightmares. Her memory brings dread and this is a disservice to her. She would not tolerate being the source of our sadness. She would line us up and smack us if she knew. She'd shake our shoulders and she'd start with you.

I am not Virginia. I never could be her kind of special, but I will try to tell you now what I believe she would under the circumstances. She might say:

I love you, Dad. I know it hasn't been easy. You're in an impossible situation, and for that, I give you endless credit. It is also true that you need someone to shake you, hard. And no one, it seems, can shake a father like his daughter.

Take off those goddamn suits.

Grow back your beard.

Bring out the sweater vests.

Grow some vegetables and support your blossoming wife like I watched her support you for over a decade.

Dad. That was not Virginia writing. That was just me. I do love you very much.

Your other daughter,
Ruth

Dear Mom:

I'm proud of you. I'm proud to even know you. If I weren't your daughter, I'd be begging for selfies with you. I am honored to have you as a shining example of what a woman with an iron will might accomplish.

Also, I am disappointed in you.

This, I know, will be hard to read, but you abandoned us for greater causes. You ran, not only from your own grief, but from the heavy lifting of helping your loved ones work through grief.

Like it or not, you were equipped to help and you eliminated yourself from the equation.

Years from now, I may view this choice as brave. But today, I feel like an unchecked box at the bottom of your long to-do list. Melody and Dad and me and Virginia...unchecked and pushed to a calmer day on your calendar that never came.

I want to pause here and state, for the record, that I am having trouble writing this letter to you. It's a complicated thing—to be so very proud of someone who's too busy to be there for me, for us. I don't want to pull you back down to earth, where you never belonged in the first place. I want you to fly even higher than you are now, actually. I want you to soar. But I don't want you to have to leave behind those that matter most in the process.

Does that make sense at all?

Or, maybe the real question is, is that even possible?

You're being briefed on real things that matter in the real world. Unstable zones, as Jane called them. You're holding court with kings and princes and presidents and Congress folks. Who are we to insert ourselves in such important work? We're, dare I say, nobody—me, Dad, Melody—absolutely no one in comparison to kings and queens.

The more I write this, the more I feel guilty writing this.

I guess the fault lines aren't clear enough yet to assign blame in any particular place. But one thing is for sure. I feel...well, left behind. I think

I can speak for Melody and say that she does, too.
As for Dad, mixed in the jealousy and anger and all
of it, he does, too.

And Virginia.

She was . . .

I swear I was going to write something else
after that but I can't think of it. Actually, it may
not be that important. Maybe, the most important
thing is that Virginia WAS.

She died, Mom.

I stopped writing because I knew, sooner or
later, I'd have to write that Virginia was . . . She
told me to write the truth. She begged me the day
she died. She charged me. And after that day, the
truth undeniable is that she died. She no longer
is . . .

She was.

I need to admit that I have not accepted
anything about this yet. I also need to admit that
I am a hypocrite for the following statement, but
still, here's the statement:

Accept that your eldest daughter, Virginia
Marcie Fitz, is dead. Stop running away from that
fact or you will run face-first into a concrete wall
of despair. Try walking. Then sitting. And then,
maybe, a child's pose. Whatever you choose, stop
running. It won't help.

I'll end this letter in the same way I started it by saying I am proud to know you. I am proud to be your daughter. I am not sure if I'm worthy to be your daughter. Still, I am proud.

Ruth

Melody, my love:

Ah, I've held myself together through the first two, but here come the tears.

I must keep this short, my love. For you, I write a poem. Which, in my humble opinion, is reserved for only the highest royalty.

RUG AT THE FOOT OF THE BED

Small. Mighty. Expansive. Powerful. Girl.
If I could, Love, I'd give you the whole
    world.
On a platter with dainty flags,
Brie. Ritzy. Delicacies. Time. Attention
    uninterrupted.
You deserve more than a rug at the foot of
    the bed.
On a hard floor.

You. Small. Mighty. Expansive. Powerful.
Girl.
Deserve the whole wide world.

I cannot make it, Melody. I cannot finish this letter. Or this poem. I can no longer see through my eyes.

Yours and forever yours
as long as you'll have me,
Ruuuuuuuu

35

I heard another damn knock on the door. "Ready for Trevor?" Jane asked and then went silent. "You okay in there?" She must've heard me crying. "I'll let him have a solo session with Judy for a few minutes. Come out when you're ready."

Though Jane knocked more than anyone I'd ever known, she was growing on me. She was a multilayered person, certainly. Easy to write off as an annoying go-getter of a know-it-all, but she cared. I could see it and I wondered who else saw it, too.

Lifting myself from bed felt like lifting a car. I looked in the bathroom mirror and turned the shower to the hottest setting. Steam fogged the bathroom and I wrote *you're writing again* on the bathroom mirror.

I stood naked in the bathroom staring at the three words written.

WRITTEN!

I was writing again.

As far back as I could remember, I'd written. With such a loud, passionate family, it was a way to express myself. Expel my innards through fingertips, sometimes to just crumple the pages and trash them. Writing gave me a way to give it all away.

I'd stopped cold for Virginia . . .

Actually, I'm not sure who I'd stopped writing for. I knew Virginia would be livid at the thought. She'd curse me out for stopping. She'd fall to her knees at my feet and plead for me to write the moment, just like she had on her final day of life.

This silence was not for her at all. This was for me.

36

I lifted my naked body onto the spotless bathroom counter in the fancy hotel, crossed my legs, and wiped away the words with my forearm. Then, I gave the steam a few seconds to replenish the fog and began writing on the mirror without thinking.

ON THE MIRROR
NO WORDS
NO RETURN
NO SISTER
NO REASON TO WRITE
NO RIGHTING THE WRONG
YOU HAD NO RIGHT!
TO LEAVE ME

As I wrote forward, the topmost lines kept disappearing in the steam and I wrote faster and less coherently to try to keep up.

YOU DARE LEAVE!
PARTING WITHOUT AS MUCH AS A GOODBYE
OR FORWARDING ADDRESS
YOU KNOW HOW DAD GETS
OR MOM
YOU LEFT ME ALONE
IN A GODDAMN WIG
AND HARRIET
AND MAGIC?
I NEED YOU IN THIS BEAUTIFUL MESS
YOU!
DARE!

I didn't cry, because I was not sad. I was hot. Barely breathing in the steam and angrier than I'd felt in a long while. Every bead of sweat seeping from my pores was angry. Every damp strand of hair on my head was mad. Every bit of me.

I watched the words fog away, one by one, until the only thing left on the bathroom mirror was *YOU! DARE!* And that's why I'd stopped writing. Pure, unadulterated anger.

I closed my eyes and let it have me.

This is the moment in the story where the sympathetic

character turns bad. I didn't want that. Not for Melody. Not for Dad. Not for Mom. Not for me. Not for Virginia. But also, I didn't want to be silent anymore.

I climbed from the counter and stepped into the scorching shower. Stood underneath the unbearable hot to cool myself. Shea butter dripped into my eyes and it burned. I let it. Skin from my shoulders felt like it was peeling back and boiling. I allowed it. Sensitive breasts. Open palms. Stinging feet. I would not step away from the hurt this time, though. Feel it! Stop running from it! Exist, Ruth! Right here in the pain of boiling body and loss of a sister.

I searched myself for any other emotion hiding beneath all that mad. Sure enough, there was a tinge of something else. Something trapped tightly in the back corner of heat.

Fear.

Fear peeked out and retreated, but it was too late, I'd already seen it. I turned down the hot water fraction by fraction by fraction. It was still hot. I stood under the stream, searching now for something other than anger or fear.

And finally, there it was. Joy.

"How did you get in there?" I said, laughing. Tasting shea butter from my hair and comforting hot water from the Peabody.

And then, my mind flashed sweet visions of my sister Virginia. Moments I'd locked off as soon as Twitter told me she was gone. The vivid memory of Virginia introducing me to all of her many friends as the baby sister who would change the world one day. I smiled at the fact that no one in her friend group believed that. I saw their faces. I felt the internal rolling of doubtful eyes. But also, I knew that Virginia, my sister, believed it with her whole heart.

My sister believed I could be an actual storm, not just a quiet one.

I turned off the water, stepped out of the shower, and took a seat back on the bathroom counter in front of the mirror.

DEAREST VIRGINIA:

I THINK I JUST STARED AT THE SUN AND
THE SUN FLINCHED . . .
I MISS YOU.
I WISH . . .
THERE ARE SO MANY THINGS THAT I WISH.
BUT NONE OF THEM CAN COME TRUE.
AND MY SILENCE WON'T BRING YOU BACK.
I HOPE IT'S OKAY TO TELL YOU . . .
I CAN NO LONGER BE YOUR QUIET STORM.
BUT KNOW THAT I LOVE YOU MORE THAN
EVEN WORDS.

YOUR STORM OF
ANOTHER SORT,
RUTH

37

Rifling through the hotel's drawers, I found a golden pen with the Peabody inscription on it. I slipped the lace from a pair of my packed sneakers and knotted it tightly around the clip of the pen with my teeth. I looped it again and secured it around my neck where it would stay. I gently tore my mother's and father's letters from the notepad and folded them three times each. Melody's poem would stay secured in the pad. Before having too much time to worry about how they'd react to my letters, I labeled the folded notes, slipped them under their bedroom door, and went to join Jane, Judy, and Trevor in the conference room.

Jane held two thumbs in the air. "You okay?" she asked.

"I'm all right," I said, fighting the urge to nod instead of using my words.

She tilted her head, still unused to me speaking. "You sure?"

"I'm sure, Jane, thank you."

"Hello!" said Judy. "Welcome to the musicless meeting of bullet points and bore!"

"Hi, Judy," I said, taking a seat next to her.

Jane rolled her eyes at Judy and slid an iPad to me. On the screen, there was a meticulous bullet point list of public appearances including fundraisers, selfie lines, speeches, etc.

I'd never sat at a conference table before. But, for some reason, I was afraid of them. They reminded me of overly strong energy and bluster. The opposite of me.

"We were just discussing our tight schedule for the next few days," said Jane.

"Are we supposed to go to every single one of these things?" Judy asked dramatically.

"Every single one," Jane replied. "Good news is, mostly you'll just be standing there dressed nicely, and hopefully looking something close to normal. In DC, though, I need you to actually participate. But I'll be honest with you two, I'm concerned. If it goes bad, it goes bad very, very publicly and in front of influential people. Trevor." Jane turned her attention to him. "We need to come up with strong introductions for your parents . . ." Then, Jane looked at Judy picking a poppy seed from between her teeth. "Or else, we're toast."

"I can help," I said.

"Wait, what?" asked Jane.

I looked down at the gleaming wood of the conference table and lifted my chin. "I'll help with that," I said, looking over at Judy. "I think I can come up with something that fits us better than what you'd come up with. No offense, but I can make the speeches less political." I smiled at Judy. "More us."

"Huh," Jane let out in a huff and smiled. "Anyone willing to step up and take a task or two off my list is more than welcome to do that. But not this time, okay? We're expecting large donations here. Maybe one of the smaller fundraisers in the Midwest, but not this one. Besides, we have a budget for this. Plenty of professionals on staff. Thank you anyway."

"I think Wes is free to write their speeches," inserted Trevor. "He did the Sacramento set and it went over well."

"Great point," responded Jane. "Similar audience, too. He's expensive but it'll be worth it. Book him."

"Judy?" I whispered to a mischievous-looking Judy. "I think we can make that happen."

"Oh, we most definitely can."

"What was that?" Jane asked. "What are you whispering over there?"

"Oh, nothing," Judy replied.

"Okay, then," said Jane. "Well, as for the fundraiser itself, this thing is a behemoth. No pressure, but many famous people and millionaires, some billionaires, will be in attendance."

Jane paused, seemingly waiting for us to be intimidated and pull out.

"We'll be all right," I said, again stunning the room.

"My strength lies in the performance," said Judy. "Born performers shine in front of any audience."

Jane waved her hands as if gathering Judy and Trevor from the conference room. "I think we have our game plan in order. Wes will provide speeches soon and we'll reconvene to practice with Trevor."

"How long before we have to be back here for something?" I asked. "Me and Judy."

"Actually," she replied, "you have a couple hours."

"Okay," I said before turning on my heel to grab Judy.

"Exactly a couple hours! Like, you have to be in the hair and makeup chair in two hours. And don't lose the Secret Service this time. I'm trusting you guys."

"You have my word." I turned back to Jane. "And you're doing a great job here."

Jane looked near tears. "Thank you for saying that, Ruth."

I found Judy in the mini-kitchen with her father, who was whispering what seemed to be harsh instructions at her. Her head was uncharacteristically bowed forward as she stood, listening. When he noticed me watching, he scurried away like a cat-caught raccoon.

38

"South Main Book Juggler," said Judy with much less energy than she'd had moments ago in the conference room. "A little over a mile walk this way. They definitely have magnets."

We took off across the street from the Peabody. This time, dressed in basic jeans and T-shirts to look more conspicuous than the day before. Although, it didn't matter. The two Secret Service men stood out so obviously that they gave us away immediately. Still, I felt comforted by their presence. I'd truly misunderstood how many people could recognize the daughters of would-be president and vice president of the United States.

"Yesterday was nuts, huh?" asked Judy as we rushed across the Memphis streets. "That's crazier than I've ever seen it. Before that, I'd only signed a few autographs, but yesterday, Gardenia freaking Murphy fanned out. It's your mom," Judy continued. "She adds, shall we say, spirit to the campaign. She's like a spinning disco ball under a bright light. She's a superstar."

I had to again fight the urge to nod and listen without speaking. "Your dad is pretty great, too, you know," I replied. "He is the presidential nominee, after all."

"Yeah," she said with a strange fog over her voice. Not quite sadness, but something else. "He's a pretty typical politician, though. Not a star, like your mom! Please don't tell him I said that."

That last phrase made me think she might be afraid of him.

"I won't tell anyone, Judy."

I wanted her to elaborate on that. I'd seen her father's irritation when my mother took control on the phone. I thought it was run-of-the-mill chauvinism. I'd also caught a glimpse when he and my dad were bickering on their first video call. In the chaos, it'd slipped my mind. Potential conflict. Power struggle. Tug-of-war associated with a president and the second-in-command. With all of my personal family drama, I'd simply looked the other way.

Then, Judy began speaking, slower and more deliberate than I'd heard her do before. "My father doesn't like to lose," she said with both of her hands stuffed in her pockets. "He doesn't, actually, lose, I mean. He outright refuses. When I was little, he'd say that there was no point in playing any game if you didn't know you were going to win it. Once, when I was very small, he laughed in my face when he beat me at that matching game. You know the one? Where you put all the cards face down and flip to see if you remember which two match. He wiped the floor with me and laughed. I never played that game again with anyone.

"I don't know. I love my dad. He's smart, he's successful. But sometimes, I think he's kind of embarrassed that he got me as a daughter. Loony Judy. Did you know that's what they call me? I heard him say it once when he didn't think I could hear. Loony Judy."

We walked slowly and in silence, not because I didn't want to speak, but because I wanted to scream. One block of Memphis, then two, then the third.

Judy continued. "My mom hates him. She's never said it out loud, but I can tell. She hates the campaign trail even more than she hates him, so she pretends to cough and sneeze a lot. She was an actress like me. A good one. She even starred in a few seasons of *The Young and the Restless* before she got herself murdered off in order to marry my dad. No one talks about my mom anymore. No one even asks about her or where she is."

It hit me that I hadn't thought about her mom, either. Not once.

"It's weird," Judy added. "This public life. It can bring out the worst in people."

"Where is she now?" I asked. "Your mom?"

"Back at our vacation home in Sag Harbor," Judy told me. "Resting, she says, but really she's sitting in a circle with girlfriends talking smack about dear ole dad. Probably plotting his demise. Oh, please don't tell anyone any of this."

"Judy," I said, forcing her to stop walking. "Let's sit a minute."

We sat on a metal bench She looked like she'd been kicked in the heart by someone she loved very much.

The memory of the moment my mom decided to enter local politics flooded my mind as Judy and I sat quietly. About ten years back, when downtown Birmingham started to gentrify, my mom would go on long, frustrated rants at the dinner table about rising rents and hipster vibes pushing out authenticity and color. But her major point of infuriation was the school system. Virginia and I were in second and first grades at the time, but even we recognized our school was becoming cleaner and less diverse every year.

One particular night around the dinner table, Virginia stopped Mom mid-rant to suggest Mom become PTA president. Dad and I jumped on the bandwagon with encouragements and support, but as always, it had been Virginia to make the first, and most important, move. A couple months later, my mother was sworn into that very position.

Without that simple suggestion, none of this would be happening. Her ability to breathe life and encouragement into the darkest spaces. Her love, especially for those who felt unloved. Looking back now, I believe she saw my mother's untapped potential as a change agent while the rest of us saw her as the wonderful wife and mother of the Fitz household. Virginia saw her really. She saw everyone as they potentially could be.

Glancing over at Judy, I saw she needed someone like that to quiet down the naysayers and nonbelievers. She needed Virginia, but I'd have to do.

"At school, I was always picked last for everything and it never hurt my feelings," I said, before pulling my knees into my chest. "Winners were picked first. But I was glad because that meant I'd have more time to watch and write and think things through. People who win all the time tend to be more fragile than those who don't mind losing. They throw tantrums and kick things and yell out in ways I've never been comfortable doing." Judy's head was bowed. "The strongest among us are uncompromisingly themselves, whether they win, lose, or belt Broadway lyrics to unsympathetic audiences."

She laughed. "I am that—myself."

"You are," I said, looking into her sad but smiling eyes, "definitely that."

"Dads don't understand, do they?"

I thought of Harriet's scroll about the power of fathers. They really do hold their daughters' confidences in their hands. Some don't handle that power with wisdom. And Judy's, it seemed, was one who did not.

"I don't know your dad well enough to help with that," I told her. "But I do know this. You're unique. You're rare in ways that people buck against in the beginning but then love." I pulled the pen from my bra. "Wes's intro speeches for us will be generic and perfect in ways that you and I are not. Jane won't approve, but I think we should write something a bit more us. How long do we have?"

"Why is it always seventeen minutes?" she asked, laughing. "Go ahead and I'll let the guys know that we need the driver."

Judy popped up and motioned to the Secret Service. I began writing my speech first. I didn't even look at the page, I just let my hand go without thinking. I knew our introductions couldn't be long and drawn out, but those are my favorite kinds of speeches—punchy, easy to remember, to the point. The question was what would make the most genuine impact? What did Judy and I want to say to the world? Us. Not our parents, but us. Who was *our* audience?

As Judy instructed the Secret Service agents, I thought of possible answers to those questions. And began . . .

"Ride's five minutes out!" Judy jumped up from the bench and started toward the bookstore. "Magnets!"

I followed her closely, still thinking of the speeches. It was a strange thing to use my voice to speak to . . . the world. I was so used to quiet.

"That's it," I said aloud. "You go on in," I told Judy. "I have to get this thought written before it escapes my mind."

Four-and-a-half minutes later, Judy emerged with

matching Elvis magnets. Both broken and on clearance for fifty cents each. Elvis wore an orange, sparkling jacket and Judy haggled the bookstore owner down to forty-nine cents, but gave a ten-dollar tip to support the local business. I would have done the same.

We made it back to the hotel with only seconds to spare and Jane stood, tapping her foot, beside the empty makeup chairs.

"No red lip," I told her. "And no wigs."

She nodded this time instead of using her words.

I sat in the black, spinning chair and thought of how long it had been since I told someone no. Not as a question or suggestion, but as my opinion. It wasn't even that hard, the word *no*.

As the makeup artist began applying thick primer on my face, I caught sight of my father peeking out from the bedroom. When he saw that I saw him, he hid himself completely, like a skittish cat.

He'd read my letter.

I knew the letter would hurt him. He'd been through a lot. But it needed to be done. I tried to shake off creeping-in regret.

"Open your eyes," the makeup artist asked kindly. "Look up and try not to blink."

I did as I was told as she lined the inner, bottom lids of my eyes. I stared at the white ceiling with my father on my mind.

Words were too powerful. Words deserve respect; once written or spoken, words cannot be taken back. Now, my father was too ashamed to show himself. Regret began to flood my gut. I was losing the fight against it.

"Your eyes are watering," the artist said. "Do you need a break from the liner?"

I nodded and sniffled. She began tapping foundation on my cheeks and forehead and chin and I couldn't stop thinking about my aching dad.

The artist stopped completely when she realized my eyes weren't watering because of the eyeliner.

"Go take a break in the restroom," she whispered softly into my ear. "Before someone sees. Go."

I did as I was told, but my father was exiting as I was entering.

I locked eyes with him. "Hi."

"Hey." He looked at the floor.

39

He'd abandoned the suit and now wore his signature V-neck sweater vest and unwrinkleable khakis. He'd even brought out his red-rimmed glasses instead of the contacts that irritated his eyes. He looked just like my dad, only different.

"I threw out my clippers," he said. "That's what I was doing in the ... I'm trying to grow it back."

He rubbed his now-stubbly chin and grinned a bit.

"Was I too harsh?"

He grimaced. "Harsh? No. Your writing, my God. You have a way with words."

"Thanks, Dad."

"I mean it," he continued. "If a handwritten letter can reach into a man's chest and twist his heart out, phewww.

I can only imagine what's in store. You will be a master . . . what's the word for someone with such a gift?"

"Scribe," I said.

"Scribe," he repeated. "You will be a master Scribe, and soon."

"I thought you said it wasn't harsh."

"That," he said, placing his arm around my shoulders, "was a lie and you know it. But it needed to be said." He turned to look me in my eyes. "I'm sorry that you had to be the one to call me to the carpet. I am sorry for that."

"Have you talked to Mom?" I asked. "She got one, too."

His eyes widened and he shook his head slowly. "That was harsh, too?"

"Harsh and complicated."

"Well," he said. "Mind if I go check on her?"

I thought of Harriet's father building a tiny bridge for his mother to cross.

"I would love that," I told him. "And I think she will, too."

He gave me a gentle hug and then held on to my shoulders to look me over. "A master Scribe," he said. "I'm a blessed man to have such a daughter. I love you. I thank you. I'm sorry."

"It's okay, Dad," I said, speaking without counting my words. "Sometimes only a daughter can lift her father's eyelids."

He pulled me in close and held on for a very long time. "I miss Virginia," he whispered into my ear.

He'd said it. I couldn't believe he'd actually said it.

"Me too."

He kept holding me close and his tears began to fall onto my back. Right there in the ritzy hallway of the Presidential Suite, my precious father broke down. Sunny, holding Melody, rounded the opposite end of the hall and stopped when she saw us. I motioned quietly for Sunny to put Melody down and she did before silently backing away.

Melody toddled over to us, her small arms wrapping around our legs. That only made him sob harder.

Mom cracked the door of her makeshift office and all I could see was half of her face. "Sorry." She closed the door before I could tell her to join us.

And just like that, the moment was over. Dad began wiping his face vigorously with his hands, Melody lifted her arms to be picked up, and Jane started hollering from the next room.

"Fitzes!" She called out. "Where are all of the Fitzes?"

My mom eased out of the bedroom, already dressed and made-up. She waved her hand slightly but did not speak.

"You look beautiful," Dad told her.

She didn't smile. She, instead, looked very sad and exhausted. "You look like yourself." She exhaled like she was seeing something familiar and comforting that she'd long missed. Then, she looked over at me. "You're writing."

That's all she said about the letter. No elaboration.

"Ah." Jane appeared at the end of the hall. "There you all are. Ruth, makeup. Joseph, you look like Mr. Rogers. Hmm. I guess it suits you. Sunny? Come get Melody in her dress! And ma'am? Another briefing. Ready?"

We all scattered to different places in the Presidential Suite.

40

The host of the fundraiser was the wealthy owner of some type of beer company, and his driveway was long and windy with crepe myrtles perfectly spaced out alongside. The roundabout at the base of the large wooden front door was silvery cobblestone with twinkling lights peeking through the meticulous cracks.

The house—or castle, rather—had wings. Not the flying kind but the ones family members could get lost in. I imagined they needed an intercom to check in with one another.

"How many people live in this place?" Judy asked. "If you don't say twenty, it's too big!"

Jane laughed. "Two very rich and generous people live in this house. We're expecting forty more very rich and generous people to attend this fundraiser, so be on your best behavior."

"This," Trevor added, "is one of those shut up and smile occasions. No need for chitchat. You two won't even be expected to stay. You'll shake hands and welcome guests at the front door until a quarter 'til, and then Sunny will swoop in with Mel and I'll get you guys. Got it?"

"What about selfies?" asked Judy.

"What about selfies?" Trevor replied, and asked, too.

"You know they'll want selfies," Judy said, which seemed perfectly reasonable to me. "Everyone wants proof to post on social media."

"Just smile," Jane and Trevor said together as if it were the most obvious answer in the world. "Today's goal is to solidify the image of the family values candidate. Smiling children will be sufficient."

But I was right there with Judy on that one. There were thousands of variations of smiles. Wide and clownish. Small and dignified. No teeth. Teeth. Gums. A smile ran the gamut from decorous to ridiculous.

"This is our first official appearance." I had to speak up and help Judy, who was, as usual, being misunderstood. "With millionaires and a front yard the size of a football field. We need a little direction here."

Jane looked at me with pride. "Yes," she said. "Of course. I apologize for being short, Judy. It really is a reasonable request. Trevor, please demonstrate while I get the Vaseline."

Trevor started. "Here's the trick to looking interested and fresh, even when you're exhausted and ready to go to bed."

He pulled his shoulders up a few inches and tilted his head to the side. Then he stretched his lips back over his teeth and leaned into an invisible selfie partner.

"Whoa," Judy said. "That's one masterful selfie pose!"

Jane came back with a large jar of Vaseline. "Put this on your teeth. It'll help, trust me."

"Get in there, girls. And for goodness' sake, try to have a bit of fun," said Trevor.

"Thanks," Judy whispered as we stepped out of the van and into a whole new world.

Mom and Mr. Harrison were already standing at the entrance schmoozing with the hosts.

"Ahhh," Mom said with a tinge of an English accent that reminded me of Trevor's. "There they are now. Our girls."

I locked eyes with Mr. Harrison after he looked apprehensively at Judy. Then, I checked Judy and as she looked at her feet, I grasped her hand, and we joined our parents in a tight line facing the door.

"You must be Ruth," said an exceptionally dressed woman with her chignon pulled so tight that I imagined she had a headache. "I am Yolanda Pierce. You are welcome in my home."

"Thank you for having us," I said, focusing my attention on the pulse in her temples.

"And you," she said, turning to Judy. "I know you. Judith Harrison, the one and only."

Judy's eyes lit up and I could tell she wanted to put on a small show for this woman, but she looked over at her father and then at her feet.

"Yes, ma'am," Judy said. "Judith is me."

"Please send your mother well wishes," said Yolanda. "She is sorely missed. Yet again."

Judy kept looking at her feet and Mr. Harrison said absolutely nothing.

I visualized the act of turning off a bright light over and over until it finally blew the bulb. That's what Judy's father was doing to his only child—dimming her down so low that she just might break under the pressure.

"Excuse me," I said. "I have to go to the bathroom."

I broke the line before one of the parents had an opportunity to object.

"First door on the left," said Yolanda.

On the way, I grasped my pen. I didn't have paper and in the bathroom there were no paper towels. Only fancy cloth fingertip ones. I ran my hand across the fabric; it was smooth enough to hold ink so I began writing on one, and then a second, and a third.

I folded them as tightly as possible and tucked them into

my jacket pocket. Then, as if out of thin air, a scroll hit me over the head and fell into the gleaming sink.

Dearest,

This is not about me—our Scribe/Forescribe relationship—it is about you. But as I said in a previous writing, there is no guide for the guide. No special training for one charged with taking the lead. She simply does so.

A teacher is but a student who stepped forward with a raised hand. A Mother is but a daughter who had a child of her own. An enslaver is nothing but a coward whose fate has given him power.

Ah.

Pain.

This, Dearest, is why I open with the inarguable fact that this is about you! Your writing. Your voice. Your strength drawn out and into the forefront where it belongs. But of late I cannot shake trauma loose. I go to guide you and instead my ink writes of incidents in the life of me. Over centuries, I've packed

and unpacked pain a thousand times.
In the end, I think I've dropped a life
of bad onto the curb for trash pickup,
but then, all of a sudden, I realize
I've forgotten to dispose of the rubbish. I
simply refolded it back into myself where
it festers and rots.

This should not be about me. I should
answer the very astute questions you
posed in your letter, but there is no guide
for the guide. So, alas, here we are:

I was one of the only enslaved folks
in Edenton, North Carolina, with the
ability to read. My mistress taught me
when I was very young.

My mistress had taught me the precepts
of God's word. "Thou shalt love thy
neighbor as thyself." "Whatsoever ye would
that men should do unto you, do ye even
so unto them." But I was her slave, and
I suppose she did not recognize me as her
neighbor. I would give much to blot out the
memory of that great wrong.

I loved my mistress because she
provided for me the key—literacy.
She wronged me and forgiveness is a
complicated thing, but she made words

make sense, and thus, I possessed power of quiet understanding.

I see you, Ruth. Standing now in a fancy bathroom in a fancy home descended from . . . well . . . complicated things. This is where the power of quiet understanding backfires, isn't it? A beautiful Black family sent out to raise wealth deeply rooted in intentionally broken beautiful Black families. It is enough to pull out what is left of one's hair.

My solace is you. Not only you, but your intact, beautiful Black family. Mother, Father, Sisters, All Still Standing.

But to stand, you must shake a few dirty hands. I must share with you a secret I learned entirely too early in life: The dirtiest hands look clean, Dearest.

I learned this devastating tidbit from the same loving mistress who'd blessed me with words. She also promised me freedom, but in the end, I was sold to a hell I have never been able to adequately describe.

Enslavement is strategic sleight of dirty hand. A swirling cloud pretending to be puffy, white, and pure. A wolf bundled up tightly in the clothing of a precious sheep.

This letter is a mess of words so I will end with You.

I watch you, Dearest. I shed tears as I watch you rise. I ducked down for seven years on the wish that someone like you may get the opportunity to walk with your chin raised. Best of all, you're writing.

You're writing the truth whole to the masses. No colander truth with holes self—serving. But a steel bowl catching facts and nuance and all of it, there. A phoenix is emerging, Dearest. As I bear witness, I feel so much all at once that I cannot be coherent for you.

I fear, this scroll has not been at all helpful nor made any sense, but there is no guide for the guide.

I must go and write, Dearest. For myself. To sort. To organize thoughts that make no sense at all. This may take a while.

Yours,
H

I walked back to my mother's side. Smiled for selfies. Shook meticulously manicured hands. And kept reminding myself to breathe through the urge to throw up.

41

Jane stood in the bus's aisle, clipboard in one hand, phone in the other. She had been talking for a while, but I hadn't been listening.

"Next stop, Raleigh," she said, punching out a text.

"Raleigh, North Carolina?" I asked.

"So you were listening," she replied, satisfied. "That's the one."

"How far is that from Edenton?"

"I've never heard of this place." Jane's thumbs flew again to her phone. "Looks to be about a hundred and fifteen miles away. What's there?"

"Harriet Jacobs's birthplace." My dad's voice rang out confidently from the back of the bus.

I got up and joined him on the plush couch. "Mom?"

He motioned toward the closed sleeping quarters behind him. "Fell asleep as soon as we got back from the fundraiser. I had to take her heels off for her. She's exhausted."

I exhaled, worried about her.

"What do you want to know about Edenton?" he asked. "The only significant thing I know of about that town is concerning Madam Harriet."

"Harriet Jacobs," Jane said, seemingly googling. "Brave woman."

He leaned back in his seat. "Brave doesn't quite cut it when you're talking about Madam Harriet," he said, closing his eyes. "I can't imagine someone so powerful. And an iron will to set one foot in front of the other when that meant enduring unthinkable things—"

I realized that in his vest and with his stubble, Dad was beginning to look like himself.

"Well," Jane interrupted. I hadn't even realized the rest of the bus was rapt until she spoke up. "Like what?"

"*Incidents* is a firsthand account of the enslaved Black woman. Firsthand! Sure she changed names, but this may as well have been autobiography. I once measured the height and width of her crawl space for one of my classes to show them how much she had to position herself to survive. It's a heroism rarely seen in history. Her story is so incredible that it's almost unbelievable."

Everyone was listening to my father speak about Harriet Jacobs. The person who was writing to me, from ... the past? It all felt even more surreal. My father ended with the story of her finally gaining freedom. It should've been a happy story. It, however, was just as complicated as the rest.

"Madam Jacobs became a nanny to a white family in New York," he said, lost in the story. "That family bought her freedom officially for three hundred dollars."

"Thank goodness," said Frank, who was holding his heart.

"Finally," added Franny. "She could stop running."

"Yes," Dad started. "And no. Think of it! This is a woman with such internal strength that she bent body down to defy her enslaver. She counted moments, seconds, planning her ultimate escape. She'd earned her own freedom, if you ask me, by simply being born. And then, she'd earned it a thousand more times over in acts of bravery.

"In *Incidents,* she writes of bitterness about that payoff. She had the foresight not to express glee over a human being sold. It's a quiet sort of brilliance, I think. One of my favorite aspects of Madam Harriet, actually. Because she could have written paragraph on paragraph praising the family who "bought" her. Don't get me wrong, now, she expresses gratitude, but that gratitude is mixed with a foresight that no one should be allowed to buy another."

My father then calmed his flailing arms and stared me in the eye. "I was told recently, by one of the best writers living and breathing, that men can be so stupid," he said, laughing. "In so many words. Okay, not stupid. Shortsighted?"

I nodded.

"Yes," he continued. "Madam Harriet was living in a shortsighted world, surrounded by shortsighted people, with shortsighted ideas. But she saw farther. Far enough, in fact, that she refused to give another human too much credit for buying another human. And now, here I stand hundreds of years later with the unequivocal confidence that she was right. No one deserves a pat on the back for shelling out cash to buy a human being."

Hearing my father speak of a woman I'd come to know was beyond perplexing. I wanted to insert myself. I wanted to clarify a few misunderstandings and misinterpretations. Harriet would not call herself brave. She would call herself a Mother. She likely wouldn't call herself a fighter. She'd say she was a scribe, a writer with much to say.

He was correct about one thing, though: she possessed remarkable foresight. And I desperately wanted to see what she saw.

"Can we go?" I leaped up and walked over to Jane. "To Edenton. Can we please go?"

"I don't think so, guys." Jane looked at her clipboard. "We're already pushing it close as it is."

The pocket door in the back of the bus opened to reveal my disheveled mother, still in the suit from the fundraiser. She'd been listening.

"I'll tell Jim." My mother spoke with the conviction of a woman who would not be moved. "We will not be attending either of today's events. We will, instead, be taking a detour in Edenton, North Carolina."

"But ma'am," said Jane. "It's unheard of for a vice presidential—"

"I do not care at all what you are about to say next, Jane," my mother said rudely. "My family wants to visit Edenton, birthplace of Harriet Jacobs, and my family will do just that. Steven! Get us there before noon, please, so we can have a decent amount of time to tour the town." She then turned toward the bathroom. "I need a shower." She disappeared.

I felt embarrassed for Jane. I was becoming tired of my mother treating her like she wasn't doing a good job. Simultaneously, I felt for my mother, who was neck deep in pain and performance and Vaseline on teeth and expensive suits and pearls and heels and more pain and grief. She seemed untouchable. So out of reach that I couldn't budge.

"I'll go," Dad said as he got up to join her in the bathroom. "I'm concerned, too."

He followed her into the bathroom and I heard him ask if she was all right. Someone intentionally turned the water on, first the faucet, followed by the shower. They didn't want anyone to hear what they were talking about. Or maybe it was just me that they didn't want to hear.

"Ruuuuu!"

Melody, just awake from a nap, toddled into my lap and curled her warm body up like a roly-poly.

42

I don't know what I was imagining to find in Edenton. My mind's eye visualized the place woodsy with dirt roads and expansive homes. When the bus pulled in, I realized that I was imagining early 1800s Edenton, not present-day.

Now, the town was easily one of the most adorable places I'd seen in a long time. Conflict bent my belly at the thought of *adorable* Edenton. The pitch-perfect, postcard-worthy town rubbed me wrong, given its history. It reminded me of painted-over paintings.

Still, it was stunningly gorgeous surrounded by crystal waters, white picket fences, and wraparound porches on the first and second levels of homes. At one point, our bus got stuck behind a traditional green trolley with golden trim. The trolley driver pulled to the right and kindly waved us around. To the left, a red-roofed lighthouse stood at the edge of the water as sailboats leisurely glided around it and ducks sat contentedly on manicured lawns. Our bus came to a stop at a waterfront bed-and-breakfast.

"Just before noon with minutes to spare," said Steven the bus driver.

"Looks like we've got the afternoon and night off, then," said Jane, sounding completely drained. "Fitzes will be staying at the B&B. We already have a security detail assigned to the family. We'll be at the Hampton Inn down the street. If you need anything, call or text or whatever."

"Thank you, Jane," I said.

"You are welcome, Ruth."

She looked ready to call it quits.

Mom and Dad opened the pocket door and Dad motioned for the driver to take a walk with him. Sunny had already taken Melody to the room, so Mom and I were left alone on the bus. For some reason, I wanted to run away. I went to push myself up but Mom placed a firm hand on my shoulder, not quite forcing, but encouraging me to stay seated.

"Your letter," she said in a tone I could not place as positive or negative.

She sat on the couch opposite me and her head fell backward.

"Your," she said. "Letter."

"I'm sorry," I told her. Not because I was truly sorry but

because she had so much work to do. Because, as I'd said in the letter itself, I wasn't worthy of her time. She had more important things to do than sit with her daughter and talk about the effects of the campaign trail. There was legislation to write and bills to pass, elections to win.

"No, you are not." She lifted her head to stare at me. She looked full of rage and I was almost afraid of what she'd say next. "Never say sorry for utilizing your voice. When you use your words, you break through the goddamn concrete."

She fell to her knees in front of me and rested her forehead on my lap. "You are not nobody," she whispered. "You are not nobody. I am the one who should be sorry for making you feel like that."

"Mom, please. Sit up," I told her.

She did as she was told, and I sat her down to braid her wild hair. Silently. Contentedly. She sat. Eyes closed as I greased and combed her shower-frizzed hair into quick twists and pinned them into an updo.

"Now," I said, patting her gently on the head. "Let's walk."

"I've missed that," she said, stepping down and into quaint Edenton. "When you were small, both of you, I'd spend hours greasing and twisting your hair. It was my favorite part of being the mother of girls. Wash day, though? Awful!"

"When you say both of us," I started carefully. "You mean Virginia."

"I mean," she swallowed. "Yeah, her."

After my mother refused to say her name out loud, we walked in the quiet for a while. Taken by the old-world beauty of the place. Colonial homes lined the waterfront streets. Their lawns cut so meticulously that they could be straight out of a photograph. Sidewalks clean and kept. Flowers happy and blooming. The only thing that looked out of place was us, trailed by four stone-faced Secret Service agents.

"It's America," said my mom. "Very, very America. Isn't it?"

"It is," I replied. "Look at this."

We approached the visitor's center and a marker with Harriet Jacobs's name on it stood in front.

Harriet Jacobs c. 1813–1897 Fugitive slave, writer, & abolitionist. Incidents in the Life of a Slave Girl *(1861) depicts her early life. Lived in Edenton.*

My mother and I stood in the shadow of the marker. It wasn't enough for Harriet. She deserved a monument. A giant looking down on all of Edenton, not a skinny, easily missed marker. I caught sight of the giant that should've been Harriet. It was a Confederate general.

"This is also very, very America," I said to my mom.

"It is. Let's walk," she started. "I need you to tell me what to do."

"What do you mean?" I asked, concerned.

"I mean," she said, kicking small rocks as she walked. "I don't want to run anymore."

I stopped walking. "You can't drop out this late in the game. You're on the ticket. That's not possible."

"I know that," she said, kicking harder at the rocks. "I've fucked everything up, Ruth."

It wasn't a shock, hearing my mother curse, but it added intensity to the moment.

"I've fucked up my whole life," she said, kicking so hard I thought she might fall off the sidewalk. "All of it. Fucked up."

"But you're a superstar, Mom."

"A superstar to who?" she snapped. "Twitter? MS-goddamn-NBC? None of it matters when your daughter's dead."

Again, silence.

"I don't want to be famous or vice president of the United States or ride on a fucking private jet ever again, Ruth. I just want my family back." She paused to exhale and then continued. "I saw you three in the hall of the hotel. You, Dad, and Mel. I saw you. There was no space for me there. I saw you. I used to be there, too. And I fucked that up. Me."

And more silence. A few locals started pointing in our direction. I saw curtains parting and cars slow as they passed by.

"This way," I said, pulling her away from town and toward a more woodsy part of Edenton.

My mother was famous whether she liked it or not. At

that point, I likely was, too. I didn't want her to be recognized and recorded mid-meltdown. Or worse, for someone to hear her regretting her position. It would be political suicide. And so many people believed in her. I'd seen it in Atlanta and in Memphis and on the Sunday shows. Good people held out hope that my mother could change the world for the better. Maybe she could! But this would end it all and I couldn't allow that.

"Here," I said, motioning her into the woods. "Up for a hike?"

"Always," she replied, as I knew she would.

A few steps onto the trail, I caught sight of the rope-like, clinging limbs that grab ahold of tree trunks that Harriet had searched for with her father. I reached to touch them. Ran my finger down and around the thick, snug branches. I pulled at the flimsiest ones, unwrapping and pulling them loose. As we walked, I braided them in my hands.

"I bet those loafers hurt like hell," said my mother, glancing back at the Secret Service guys. "Someone should give them a raise."

"I'll tell you what to do," I said to my mother firmly. "But will you listen?"

"Ruth," she said. "I'll consider anything at this point. I'm spinning out of control."

"Okay, then. First, stop speaking to Jane and the others like they're yours to treat as horribly as you'd like. I'm not sure where that came from, but it's not you. Stress is no excuse for treating people who are helping you out like shit. They all deserve raises. They're working their asses off for you. Secondly, say your daughter's name."

I waited.

"Now."

I waited, but she wouldn't.

"When she was born, she came out singing," Mom said. "It was a strange sound and I can't completely explain it. It's one of those moments in motherhood where only you know what you know and no one else can know. She didn't cry, she sang like a bird in the morning. It's still the sweetest sound I've ever heard in my life. And I only heard it once. Your dad swears he never heard it. Anyway, I promise it's true."

"I believe you," I said. "It sounds like her."

"It does, doesn't it? I can't imagine losing a child. Even after losing one, I still can't imagine it. It's unimaginable. You know why I can't seem to say her name?" She lowered her already whispering voice. "Because I first heard it when I carried her in my body."

My mother started to cry in a silent, pained way. Her tears fell into the dirt and she stepped forward as if leaving them behind her.

"She sang me her name when she was in my womb."

That's when I spotted it, half-hidden in the thick of the woods. A little longer than three feet and curved slightly around the base of a tree. Nature had tried to take it back, wrapping it in vines and covering its back with mossy green. Two tiny mushrooms peeked through the braided wood and I had to tug with the earth to pull it free.

"My God."

"What is it?" Mom asked, standing over me.

I hadn't even realized I'd fallen to the ground by its side. It was a little bridge braided with such care and love. It was hope enduring. Ever. Lasting.

"It's love, Mom. Endless, undying, unbreakable love."

43

Dear Forescribe:

I am in Edenton.

It is more beautiful than I would have thought possible. The scars of this town have been dyed and decorated away. It is, as my mother says, very America.

I received your last letter and I have to say that I respectfully disagree with your assessment. This exchange between the two of us is not about me. This is about the both of us. As you stated very early on:

"A Black girl in 1816 and a Black girl now is not comparable. It is, how does one say instead, two sides of a rare golden coin that never made its way out of circulation. Lumpy and rough from too many transactions, this precious coin has earned a place on the mantel. Atop a silk pillow with fringe on the base. Yet, she still works her way through others' hands to get whatever it is they want from her that day. Through hands undeserving. Benefiting from her beauty, her delicacy, her will—so many do benefit, but so few respect. Rare she is, and rare she always has been. As you are, my Scribe, rare."

Yes, I have committed this passage to memory because, Dear God, to write such a paragraph. I cannot imagine writing such truth and beauty. I aspire to do it, but until then, I will memorize those of a master.

You.

This letter will be about you, Dearest Forescribe.

You.

As I breathe the air of Edenton, I feel closer to you than ever. I look out at what would have been your prison and breathe in the freshest, most pleasant air I've breathed in a long while. I feel guilty breathing in such a place. I know that I shouldn't, but I do. I feel that I do not deserve it. Because you deserved it.

You deserved dipped strawberries and grapes

without the stems. You deserved long free walks without fear of capture. You deserved, as you say, a place on the mantel atop a silk pillow with fringe at the base.

Upon your request, I have not read your masterpiece. I will continue to honor that until you tell me it is okay, but I now know more and I cannot dream up a woman more deserving of a perfectly braided bridge at her feet than you.

You.

I do not know if you sent me to your father's bridge.

I do not know what to do with it aside from hold it closely and carefully until further instruction. But as I stare at it now, I see pure love in its braids.

I see that which lasts through hurricanes and earthquakes and floods and monsters and all of it.

I see you in this bridge, Harriet Jacobs.

You.

Unyielding.

Indestructible.

Unbending, even when made to bend for seven painful years.

I see you in the carefully chosen limbs and thickets.

I hear you whispering through the twisting copse with your voice unassuming and chronically underestimated.

I feel you hurting and still pushing with all of your mighty might.

I understand you, Forescribe. More than most others ever could. The quiet power of a woman who sets pen to parchment instead of stooping herself to argue. The foresight of a human being who allows the shortsighted idiots to win small battles knowing the war will be won with a strategic narrative. The resolve.

Ah, steadfast, bidding, unmovable resolve.

I'm here for you, Forescribe, as much as you're here for me. And while, admittedly, I cannot write on your level (do not argue with me please on this because I've seen your scrolls!), I'm with you.

Your Scribe,
Ruth

44

Breakfast was served by the sweet-natured owner of the bed-and-breakfast. She kept staring at my mom and looking away quickly as if not to get caught. She wanted a selfie badly and she was too respectful to ask.

"These pancakes are delicious," my mother told her, and the woman looked like she might faint. "Do you share recipes?"

"On-on our website," the woman stuttered. "But I think I have a copy printed in the back. Here, I'll go get it for you."

As the woman nearly tripped over her feet turning the corner, my dad said, "For goodness' sake, Velicia, offer that poor woman a selfie."

I laughed and so did Mom. Then Melody did, too.

"Can I finish eating first, Jo?" my mom asked my dad, intentionally using his nickname.

"Maaaaama!" Melody yelled out and then smiled so widely that we all melted down to her.

"Good job, Babe," I told her.

She looked over at me. "Ruuuuuuu!"

"That's right," Dad said, obviously hoping she'd call out his name next.

"Daaaaaada!" she obliged, and we were all happy for the first time in a long time.

When the lady returned, she looked flustered. "Have you all seen?"

"Oh no," said my mom, obviously expecting the worst. "What now?"

The phone Jane had given me began to vibrate. I had no idea where it was since I rarely looked at it. Dad's cell started ringing, too, and then Mom's.

"Shall I turn on the news?" asked the lady. "Or would you rather finish enjoying your breakfast before?"

Mom motioned her to turn it on and so she did.

"My God," said Dad.

45

A video of my father being arrested years earlier ran on a loop with the Breaking News banner flashing. The quick description underneath read "Joseph R. Fitz officially fired from professorship for lying on app."

"What's this?" he asked no one in particular. "What exactly is this?"

We all looked at him without answering. Even Melody watched him with apprehension and concern. The anchorwoman on the news began talking.

"Video of the 2004 arrest of Joseph Roderick Fitz, husband of the Democratic vice presidential nominee, has been leaked to our station," the anchor started as if she weren't breaking people's lives apart with every word. "He has been let go from his prestigious professorship and department head position as of this morning. We'll be reporting on this as we gather more information."

Dad switched to another network. The red Breaking News banner flashed again and the description underneath was worse. So horrifying, I couldn't believe a reputable news station would report it. But there it was.

"Video of VP nominee's deceased daughter's drug activity leaked."

We watched beautiful, laughing Virginia surrounded by friends with blanked-out faces. She wore her favorite sunflower baby doll dress and I could hear Pink Floyd playing in the background. A quick flash of jealousy flew across my belly at the sight of her sharing our secret songs with people I hardly knew, but it disappeared as quickly as it came.

She'd tucked a dandelion in one of her braids. She smoked and giggled and giggled some more. Innocently. Sweetly. Hurting no one at all. Alive. I smiled at the video for a few moments. This was my sister, perfectly represented. She was joy. But then, the horrible anchors took control of the narrative.

"What kind of thugs are we considering electing to the second highest office in the United States of America?" one asked another. "Illegal drugs, arrests, child abandonment? These people should be nowhere near the White House."

"I agree, Todd," replied the stiff-haired blond woman on the panel. "I'm old enough to remember Washington having family values. This is unacceptable."

I tried to mute them out and hone in on *Dark Side of the Moon* playing softly in the background.

Jane burst into the front door of the bed-and-breakfast looking absolutely horrified. "Mr. Harrison would like a conference," she told my mother. "We need to fix this now. Sunny, get the baby. Frank, Franny, pack up everyone's stuff for the bus. We need to get everyone loaded within the hour. We've got DC next."

"Ma'am?" She cautiously handed my mother the phone. "Sorry, but you need to talk to Mr. Harrison."

"What did he mean?" Mom asked, looking off in the distance, "by child abandonment? He meant me. Of course, he meant me."

"Jane," Dad interjected. "I understand this is your job. But we need a minute as a family. Sunny, let Melody down. Jane, ten minutes, you can time us. And ma'am," Dad motioned to the bed-and-breakfast's owner. "Could you give us privacy, please?"

Everyone bowed out of the dining room, leaving us to ourselves.

Melody began poking at Mom's pant leg. "Maaaaaaama!"

Mom lifted her and Melody tucked her head into the nook of Mom's chin and shoulder.

Silence.

Dad looked lost in his own pain. Mom looked as if someone had reached into her aching heart and removed it from her body. And Melody looked concerned. This was our pattern. Quiet when something desperately needed to be said. Running when everyone needed to stand still. Stillness when action was necessary. All we had was ten minutes. Ten measly minutes! To merge as a united front in the face of the world's chaos. Ten fucking minutes. To figure out how to weather this storm together. Ten minutes, nine now. But no one budged. No one spoke up. No one took control of the moment.

Melody lifted her head and stared into my eyes. She smirked knowingly as if pushing me to the front of the line. She nodded and said, "Ruuuuuuu."

She and I both knew that it was up to me.

"Listen," I said. "We don't have long to figure this out. There's no way around this. No way under it or over it. We have to walk through this together. I need information, first, and we don't have long."

And because old habits die hard, I began counting. That'd been almost forty words. Just there in the introduction. I wanted to fix this. I wanted to speak like Melody wanted me to. They stared at me—Mom, Dad, Mel—like I could do something about this. I really could. I knew how to help, but my mouth wouldn't open. I was no fixer. But I knew someone who was.

"Jane," I told them. "We need Jane."

"This is a family affair," injected Dad.

"Trust me?" I pleaded. "We need Jane. Now."

He nodded, then Mom, and Melody said, "Ruuu."

When I opened the door, Jane nearly fell inside. "Please come."

Jane's eyes doubled in size as she awkwardly accepted my mother's seat at the breakfast table.

"Jane," I began. "I need you to do your thing, okay?"

Jane squared her shoulders and lifted the master iPad from her bag.

"Dad, quick, what were you arrested for?" I asked, shaking off the longing to count.

"Protests," he replied. "I'd do it again."

"Got that, Jane?" I asked.

"We can spin that," Jane said without looking up from her typing.

"Mom?" I looked over to her. "Do you feel like you abandoned your family? Sorry to ask like that but we only have seven minutes left."

She nodded and hugged Melody in closer. "I do."

"Should I?" Jane asked, motioning toward the door.

"No, Jane," my mother softly replied. "Stay."

"Okay," I said. "You kind of did. Dad, do you agree with us that Mom dipped when she shouldn't have?"

"I do," he said to her. "I'm sorry."

"No," she injected. "I'm sorry."

"Well, then," I replied. "Everybody agrees. Everyone's sorry. Now what?"

No one spoke, so I continued. "Now, we make a decision. Either we wallow in it for the rest of our lives, or we let it go so we can take this shit on together. Look." I pointed at the now-muted television. "The bastards are trying to attack Virginia."

"Giiiiiinnniaaaaa!" Melody yelled out angrily.

"They dare," I said. "They messed with the wrong Fitz when they messed with Virginia."

I saw my dad's nostrils begin to flair and my mother's eyes narrow. Yep. They'd done it now. The motherfuckers had done us a favor, actually, in attacking the dead love of our lives. They united us. They made every other failure within our unit insignificant. This was Virginia they were talking about.

"Thank you, Jane," Mom told her, "for those few moments. Now set up the call with Harrison."

"Where should we do this?" Jane asked.

"Right here," Mom replied. "With all four of us on the call."

46

Mr. Harrison's worried face appeared on the screen. He was alone on the presidential campaign bus with his chin in his hand.

"Oh," he said, seeing all of us clumped together in the frame. "I'd only expected, huh, nice to see you all again."

"Is it?" Dad asked rudely, and I shot him a look.

"It most certainly is, sir," Mr. Harrison replied. "The circumstances are not ideal. I wish you all would have joined us at yesterday's fundraiser. Jane said you took a bit of a detour. My wife actually showed up this time and I was left alone to schmooze with her and Judy."

He said it like it was a joke. His family. A joke. But no one laughed because it was the opposite of funny.

"Okay, then," he continued. "Jane has just informed

me that your bus driver, Steven, is the one who leaked the information to the media."

"Damn," said Dad, and the rest of us remained quiet.

"Damn is correct," Mr. Harrison replied. "Also, Jane's now-former assistant Harold sold the video of your Virginia."

"Knew I never liked that little fucker," said Dad.

"Both have been let go and we're looking into their NDAs and what-all damage was done. Steven especially had access to conversations and interactions, so I need to know if anything was discussed in front of him that will cause more, how do I say, embarrassment?"

We looked at one another, still reeling from the news that had already come out.

"Not that we can remember at this time," said my mother. "No."

"Tonight," Mr. Harrison went on, "we have a major fundraiser. None of us can miss this event after today's bombshells. It will look like political dodging and we must face these things head-on. Do you all understand?"

Of course we understood.

"Game plan will be"—he sighed—"make it through to the next news cycle. Until then, we'll just have to grin and bear it. Everybody good with that?"

We nodded as a family but I could feel him rubbing us all the wrong way.

"Jane," he called out. "On the drive up, let's give the

Fitzes some tools on riding out scandal. No interviews. Bare minimum is the best play right now."

"Yes, sir," Jane replied off camera.

"Goodbye, all."

He hung up and Jane took the phone. "He's wrong," she said, and we were all surprised. "This is bigger than grin and bear it. This is racial. I mean," she continued, "isn't it obvious? The unreasonable arrest of a Black man protesting. Accusing a hard-working badass Black mother of abandonment. Attacking your deceased daughter for smoking a little weed and listening to Pink Floyd. This is some bullshit. Sorry, Melody, but this is some absolute fucking bullshit."

Dad looked around to all of us. "We agree."

"I know this isn't my place to speak here but I also agree," said the bed-and-breakfast owner from the back corner of the dining room. "Fucking bullshit."

Mom stepped forward and held her hand out for the woman's phone. "Selfie?"

"Yes, please."

47

"I'll drive the bus," Franny announced as we all gathered in the B&B parking lot. "What? My mom drives for Greyhound. I grew up with it."

"Badass," said Frank, impressed. "I did not know that."

"It's just a little over an hour away," Jane said, looking up from her phone. "We need to huddle, all of us. I'll conference Trevor in—he's been on the road with Judy. I'll make sure she doesn't know."

"Judy should be conferenced in, too," I said firmly.

"Uh, I don't understand," Jane said, ushering everyone onto the bus. "She'll tell her father what we're up to. And we've already had one rat in our midst. Mr. Harrison can't know what we're about to do. We'll all be fired. Maybe even your mother."

"Judy won't tell," I said without a single doubt. "Jane, you need to trust me when I say Judy adds more than you can see with your eyes."

"When my daughter says trust her," Dad interjected as he stepped up and into the bus, "do yourself a favor and trust her."

"All right," Jane said apprehensively. "I'll text Trevor to loop her in. If you're sure."

"I'm sure," I said.

I was the last one to step onto the bus. I took a moment to take it all in. Franny driving this enormous beast as if she owned it. Frank sitting directly behind her in absolute awe. Sunny lifting my pride and joy, Melody, high over her head. Mom and Dad sitting together on the plush back couches, almost leaning on each other. And Jane bringing up the rear. I loved this group of folks.

"Everyone on?" asked Jane. "Shut the door and let's get going, Franny."

Everyone sat except for Jane, who began pushing more hidden buttons on the bus. Some seamlessly transformed regular chairs into loveseats and other buttons twisted them around so that they created a buffet-style setup. The last button parted the floor and a table slowly rose.

"Come on, everyone," she said finally. "Gather around. We don't have long to get a game plan going. Trevor, are you there?"

"I'm here!"

"Judy? How about you?"

"Here, but I need to whisper so my dad doesn't hear."

"Understood," said Jane. "First, ma'am, how do you feel about doing immediate interviews?"

Mom smiled. "I can get *Lillian Tonight* on within the hour."

"What about the other, less sympathetic networks?" she asked. "Todd and Tracy have been especially vicious today."

"I can take them," Mom replied, and I was proud but not surprised. This was her wheelhouse. "Need me to call Lillian now?"

"Yes, ma'am."

Mom pressed a single button on her phone. "Yes, Lillian?" She got up and disappeared behind the pocket doors.

"Judy," Jane continued. "Where are you with memorizing the speech? It's been a bit chaotic, so I haven't had a chance to check in on that. Trevor forwarded those two speeches to your iPads."

"We'll be reading our own," I said.

"I'm ready," Judy whispered. "Been working on it all night."

"What?" Jane asked me, concerned.

"Trust me," I replied with a wink.

"Trust her," Dad added.

"Trust isn't in my nature, but this whole train is off the rails at this point. May as well use your own words," said Jane. "How do you feel about your own speech?"

"Good to go."

Mom reopened the pocket door. "Just prerecorded with Lillian. It will air in about fifteen minutes. Reached out to Todd and Tracy. I'll do that live in forty-five. It's video, so I'll need—"

"On it." Frank leaped up, grabbing his train case and garment bag. "I'll get you together right here."

Frank began by wiping Mom's face clean and rubbing lotion into her smooth skin.

"Fitzes," Jane said with a new somber voice. "How would you like to address this? I cannot provide any advice here. I know my limits. This is something I do not understand and I will not pretend to. Trevor, you can help with delivery but the message and response must be from you guys. This is blatant racism against a Black family. Full stop. And we have"—she looked at her watch—"fifty-seven minutes to figure out a plan of action. Any ideas?"

No one jumped right in. So I did.

"We tell it like it is," I said. "The truth is the only way. Confront it head-on."

"Agreed," Trevor said via video conference. "But how exactly do you confront such nastiness head-on without cursing? You all deserve to, by the way. I know that isn't helping but it's the truth."

I reached out and held my palms open for my mom and dad to hold my hands. "As a united front, that's how. Melody, too. Frank, did you bring my cream suit by chance?

I say we dig it out at the root. I say we go on *Todd and Tracy* together as a family."

After a pause, Jane said, "No way. They'll annihilate you."

"Oh, I'd like to see them try."

"Jane?" Trevor asked. "Think about it, though. Their attacks have been personal. They certainly aren't fighting fair."

"But nothing like this has ever been done before . . ."

"That doesn't mean it shouldn't be done now," Trevor argued. "This isn't about winning or losing an election. This, guys, is about a party that knows it's losing, abandoning all decency, and relying on racial bullshit. If you feel comfortable enough to face those fuckers, do it. This is about more than politics."

Jane stared at the roof of the bus, thinking it through. I could see the wheels turning between her job and her beliefs. From what little I knew about politics, I knew that curveballs, especially this late, were frowned upon. Defying the would-be president was one thing, but changing the whole game was quite another.

"What if they're vicious?" Jane asked the ceiling. "What if they unleash on you all? What if they humiliate you? And Mr. Harrison, I'm sure you've all gathered, can be . . . unreasonable when backed into a corner. His team is attempting to manage this by deflecting, shifting, and shuttering. They're missing the moment on purpose, because they know this makes him look like you're the nominee for president, not the other way around. Guys"—she paused to really look at us individually—"this will come from all sides."

"Jane," I said, "no offense, but you obviously don't know the Fitzes."

48

Jane had to silence her phone as she rearranged the bus again, giving the four of us a long couch to sit on for filming. Frank set up the tripod and manipulated the lighting perfectly.

"You ready for this?" Jane asked for the thirteenth time. "Let's go. Three, two, one . . ."

"Joining us tonight," said the perfectly made-up, blonde anchor, Tracy. "Velicia Fitz, oh what a treat. And her beautiful family. I had no idea. Todd? Were you informed that we'd be interviewing the family in its precious entirety?"

The anchors known as Tracy and Todd looked extremely annoyed by the blindside and I knew then it was a good idea after all.

"No, not at all. What. A. Treat," he said with a saccharine tone. "Introduce yourselves, why dontcha?"

"I'm the senator's husband, Joseph; these are my daughters, Ruth and Melody; and you referred to Senator Fitz as Velicia. Wouldn't you think it more appropriate to call her by her title? That is why you invited her here, isn't it?"

"Oh yes," Tracy replied. "Senator Fitz, my apologizes for the complete misspeak. And you're absolutely right, Mr. Fitz, we only invited her here. So, pardon me, but why has your whole family tagged along? Seems a tad bit fame-seeking to me. I beg your pardon again, but I owe my audience candor."

My dad looked over at my mom as if requesting her approval to continue speaking.

"Go ahead, Jo," Mom said, and I smiled because I couldn't help it.

"Fame-seeking?" Dad laughed. "Oh no. Justice-seeking, more like. I've been watching your racist attacks on my family all day long—"

"Oh, I beg your pardon," Tracy interrupted. "But no one here has a racist bone in their—"

"Karen?" Mom charged right back at her.

"It's Tracy."

"Okay," Mom continued. "Tracy. Do not interrupt my husband again."

The woman looked like she'd been hit with a stun gun.

"As I was saying." Dad started again. "I've watched you

try to create a despicable narrative about my Black family. A ridiculous one that would be easily fixed with a short Google search. My arrest is a source of pride, Karen."

"Tracy."

"Tracy," he said. "I was arrested to bring attention to the slaying of innocent men, women, and children in Darfur. I carry that arrest record as a source of dignity, not shame. The fact that my university was so quick to release me from service without as much as an inquiry is abysmal and they should be embarrassed. I will never go back to that professorship, even when they offer to reinstate me as department head, which they undoubtedly will after this interview airs. Senator and future Vice President Velicia Fitz can speak for herself as for her parenting, but I cannot pass on the floor without saying this about her.

"She is, Tracy, the best example of a woman that any man breathing could ask for as the mother of his daughters. She leads with integrity and strength. She holds court with imbeciles such as yourselves without flinching, I beg your pardon. She is a queen and she deserves your respect and your apologies. So do my daughters, Ruth and Melody. Lastly, if you, or any of your dumb fake breaker broadcasters dare speak the name of my deceased Virginia, so help me I will hunt you down—"

"Jo," Mom interrupted. "Live TV, Babe."

He cleared his throat. "I was done anyway."

Mom placed her hand on Dad's thigh. "I love you," she told him.

"I love you, too," he said before kissing her quickly, right there on television.

Todd raised his hand. "May I say something?" he asked as if it wasn't his own show. "I have never had a racist thought in my life. And I never approved any discussion about your firing. That's not our call. That's production's choices. I was sent a video of you in handcuffs and if you were white, I would've done the same exact thing. The race card isn't necessary here. And I never called the senator a bad mother. You misunderstood. This is just a misunderstanding—"

"Stop," I said before anyone else had an opportunity to speak. "We watched you trash our family. We're sitting here now having to defend ourselves from a narrative you're trying to create. A narrative so many other Black families don't have the platform to fight against, but here we are. And you, Todd and Tracy, you've been called to the carpet by a family who refuses to be labeled a bunch of thugs. Your words, Todd. You called an African American history professor, a sitting senator, and their underage daughters, one of them dead, Todd. You! You called us thugs. Stop pretending. You have no plays left. Game over. Your narrative does not stand.

"We are an American family trying our best to make this world a better place. We're taking hits that white families don't take. And we aren't going to quietly stand by and allow you to tell the world who we are. You chose the wrong ones to mess with this time."

Quiet.

"Well," said Todd. "That's all the time we have this evening for ... what's this called again? *Todd and Tracy Talk About the Day.* We'll see you all tomorrow."

"We still have thirty-minutes," Tracy said through a fake, plastered-on smile.

"Get us off!" Todd yelled over the camera. "Now!"

49

We pulled into Washington, DC, before five o'clock and there was a sea of cameras waiting at the hotel. The Todd and Tracy interview went viral immediately. Jane watched our socials in real time and Mom's following grew by thirteen million in the span of the fifteen or so minutes we were on the air.

Jane wouldn't stop refreshing our stats on Twitter. Six million mentions, no, six-point-two, my God, ten million mentions. "This is unheard of," she said. "Ruth, you're a genius."

Dad looked out at the cameras. "How are we supposed to get out of the bus safely?"

"You're right. Our regular Secret Service detail won't be enough. I'll have more added," Jane said, lifting the phone to her ear. "Yeah, it's us. We need a clear path. We have a baby with us so I mean a clear path straight to the private elevators." She hung up. "They'll be here in a few minutes to get us."

"That's Jim," my mom said, refusing his call again. "He's pissed."

"Yeah," replied Jane. "His entire team has been trying to get through to me, too. Since you all shut it down on Todd and Tracy."

"You're eclipsing him," said Franny from the driver's seat. "Isn't that the elephant in the room?"

"It's his own fault, really," said Frank. "I tried to convince him to put on an interesting tie or something. He nearly bit my head off. He's as bland as they come."

And as if on cue, Harrison stepped out of the hotel, waving and smiling. The crowd of camerapeople converged on him and he stopped to take questions. Everyone on the bus quieted down to listen in.

"Hello, hello, hello," he said with his signature forced hokeyness. "So glad to be back in our capital city."

"Did you see Senator Fitz's interview?"

"How do you feel about their accusations of racism?"

"Do you agree with them?"

"Have you heard that your running mate is trending significantly higher than you?"

"Oh." He laughed with a *ha ha ha*. "Is she, now?"

"The racism, sir. How do you feel about that?"

"Do you support Senator Fitz's family in this campaign?"

"Of course I support Senator Fitz's family," he said, seemingly offended and grasping his heart. "I think of them as my own family, actually. When they hurt, so do I. And as for racism, in any form whatsoever, it will not be tolerated."

"How will you combat racism in your own campaign?"

"I will publicly and loudly condemn it in all forms. Thank you and God bless America."

Then he walked forward toward our bus, still waving and smiling.

"That's it?" Dad asked. "Huh."

"Here he comes," said Jane, ducking in her seat.

Mr. Harrison rose into the bus, smile gone and a scowl replacing it. He silently stared at Jane, then my mother, then my father, and then me.

"That was an impressive display. Reckless, but impressive." He walked up the aisle and then turned on his heel to pace back to the front of the bus. "But, as you all know, I am the head of this campaign. I chose you"—he spoke directly to my mother—"so I expect to be in the loop when such large decisions are made."

My father stood to argue, but ten police escorts cleared a way for us to exit the chaos and they were motioning us off the bus.

"See you all at the fundraiser," said Mr. Harrison. "No surprises." He stepped down, waving and showing all of his white teeth to the crowd.

50

Frank and Franny put me in a floor-length sequined blue gown. They clipped an intricate rhinestone side comb into my loose afro and painted my lips pink instead of red.

"You look," said Judy, bowing dramatically, "splendid."

"As do you," I said, bowing back to her. "Are you ready for tonight?"

"As I'll ever be."

I gave her shoulder a quick squeeze. "Be right back."

I needed a moment to sit with my introduction speech so I went to my bedroom. The scroll was on my pillow next to a heart-shaped piece of dark chocolate.

Dearest,

I will answer your questions:

Yes, I am real.

No, you are not insane.

Yes, I have met your Virginia.

No, she did not send me to you.

Why you, I will save until the end.

Next question, I think, was am I dead. Of course.

Yes, you may call me Harriet.

What I want from you is to step into your potential.

The next question, I love. It is about the story of the bird fighting with the sun. You asked, Dearest, if I was that bird. No, but I used to be. Oh, for years and years, I was. I fought until I couldn't fight any longer. I've had my turn to stare at the sun for myself.

You are that bird now, and you will have a long life so you will have to make the choice many more times—cower in the face of it or stand and fight like hell.

Next question. Are you possibly worthy? Yes. You are worthy of more than this pitiful world could ever offer you. You are worthy of . . . more.

Will you ever not fear the sun? That I do not know. I cannot see the future, after all, but I will say this. The actual sun should be feared. Fore it is hot and angry. But beware, Dearest, because especially for us Black women and girls, there are fake suns attempting to burn us at every turn. They pretend to be hot and terrifying. Do not waste time fearing them. Never cower to them. They cower only to you.

Now, for your last question—why you.

I saved it because . . . Ah, you.

Ah, formidable, potent, steadfast, resolute, unswerving You.

Why. _You_?

There will never be enough words to answer that two—worded, insurmountable question. You're the hopes and dreams of generations of women. You're the embodiment of millions of unattainable wishes. You're made of daydreams and pipe dreams and castles in the air. You're a long—held sigh finally let out by your ancestors. You're glasses on the face of those who were not allowed to see before you. You're the skeleton key to unlock all lingering chains. You're wings unclipped. You're thirst doused. You're feet rested after a long journey. You're seven trees planted from seed finally bearing fruit. You're a dip in the pool without lustful watching eyes. Freedom. That's what you are. Words, too. Freedom and words. You're words strung together to draw venom from the veins of those of us still aching.

    You.

    Are.

    <u>Words!</u>

    Why you . . .

    Why you . . .

    Ha! Such a ridiculous question.

                    Your Forescribe,
                    Harriet

51

Thankfully, the fundraiser was in the hotel. Still, our Secret Service detail insisted we leave the suite in chunks. A large group of men surrounded Mom, Dad, and Melody first, then Judy and me several minutes later. There are hundreds of press folks here, they said, and they get crafty when the story's hot enough.

We're the hot-enough-story, I thought. From ambiguous brownstone in Birmingham to the hot-enough-story. It was mind-blowing how fast politics could sweep a family into its vortex. Welcome to the machine, I guess.

"I'm nervous," Judy said when we were the only ones left in the giant hotel suite. "I want to do justice to the speech you wrote for me. I cried when I read it for the first time."

I sat for a second to think. Everyone I'd allowed into my writing life lately was telling me the same thing—they were, in some way, affected by my words. They seemed to respect my craft, even respond emotionally to it. I decided, then and there, never to stop writing again. Never to stop speaking, either. Never to hide my magic away.

I placed my hand on Judy's knee. "Actually, I think we make a good team. I write. You perform. Just do what you were born to do and it will be astonishing."

"My dad told me to stop talking so much," she said sadly. "After Memphis, he pulled me aside and said I was embarrassing him. He didn't use those words, but I caught his drift."

I turned to her. "Forgive me for saying this?" I waited for her to nod before I continued. "But your father has no idea how wonderful you are. Just as you are. Not muted or calmed down. I figured he spoke to you about something because you haven't been yourself. But promise me something? At least for the span of this three-minute speech, be you. For all we know, we've already tanked the campaign." I laughed. "I hope that's not true but who knows? This could be your last opportunity to speak in front of a crowd of prominent people. A Broadway producer could be out there! In this moment, you'll be introducing your father to speak, that's true. But the microphone is yours as long as you have it. Make it special."

"Consequences be damned?"

"Consequences be damned," I replied. "What's the worst he could do? Be disappointed? Disappointed seems to be his due north anyway. No point walking on eggshells with your father any longer. You've got a fabulous life to live. Let this be your debut."

Judy popped up and spread her arms open. "You're right! This shall be my debut."

"That's my girl," I said as the Secret Service cracked open the main door of the suite.

"It's time," they said. "Ready?"

Judy bolted toward them. "Break a leg, Ruth."

"Break a leg, Judy."

52

If there's one thing I noticed about rich people, it's that they are obsessively particular about food. Impeccably dressed waitstaff carried whole lobsters on platters, smelly cheeses, and steaks that seemed to be cut with precision lasers. More food framed the perimeter of the place— towers of flowing chocolate fondue, a large leg of lamb— there was even a table specially set with a wide variety of olives. Stranger still, no one seemed to be eating any of it. It was there for decoration and aroma while the attendants glided here and there in their fancy clothing.

I felt a poke to my shoulder. "Hey," said an unfamiliar male voice. "Boss said I wasn't supposed to say anything, but you were amazing today. Thank your family for me."

And then he walked off to offer another guest a spot of

brie. He looked back over his shoulder at me briefly. If I had to guess, I'd say he was in his early forties, a thin Black man with tears in his eyes. He disappeared into a clump of wealth, and he was gone as quickly as he had come.

"Ladies and gentlemen," Jane said from the stage. "Make your way to your seats, please. We have a phenomenal program for you all. As you're walking, I'd like to reintroduce our incredible band, and as a special treat, Tyler Davis, the most recent winner of *Idol*, will join them. Enjoy! And do not forget, the silent auction is available until midnight. Mrs. Northrip has kindly donated a Tesla to the roster as of a few moments ago. If you would like to bid on that, you'll have to do a write-in. Fifteen-thousand-dollar increments only on that one. Thanks!"

The band played "A Change Is Gonna Come" by Sam Cooke, accompanying Tyler. It always rubbed me wrong when a white person sang that song. I wondered if I was the only one. I searched the room and saw the waiter who'd poked me shaking his head at the singer in disgust. That made me chuckle to myself.

I took my seat as Mom and Dad finished their schmoozing. I must say, Dad seemed to be stepping into his new role as Second Gentleman to Be. He stood by Mom as famous people littered her with a plethora of questions. To his credit, if he was uncomfortable, I saw no sign of it. He looked like a centaur standing guard.

Mr. Harrison was the first to join me at the head table. "Well, hello there, Ruth."

"Hi."

"I've been meaning to thank you," he said.

Intrigued, I said. "For what, exactly?"

"You've been a good influence on my Judy," he said smugly, leaning in. "Encouraged her to mind her words. You excel at that yourself—well, most of the time."

My parents took their seats to my left, followed by Sunny and Melody. "Hi, Ruth," my mother interjected. "Everything okay here?"

She shot a stern glare toward Mr. Harrison.

"Oh yes," he said. "We were just chatting about knowing the value of thoughtful expression."

"You okay?" My mother asked me.

"I am," I replied.

"Wait one minute here now," said Mr. Harrison, who'd been looking over the program on the table. "In what world does the vice president speak after the president? I'm supposed to close this thing out. That's how this works. Who put this program together?"

"Where is Mrs. Harrison?" my mother asked, wisely not acknowledging his absurd whining at all. I was beginning to understand why my mother was so incredibly stressed. She'd been wrangling the head of the ticket like a child, likely for weeks.

"She's ill," he replied shortly. "No longer up for the rigor of it all."

"Feel free to continue eating," Jane said, again onstage. "We're going to get started with the ever-entertaining Judith Harrison introducing the next president of the United States, Jim Harrison. Help me welcome this multi-talented young lady to the stage!"

Judy cautiously stepped up to the microphone and tapped it. "This thing on?" she asked, chuckling, and I watched Mr. Harrison cringe in his seat.

"My father is a winner." She stopped talking to stare at him and smile. "That's what Jim Harrison does, he wins. I've known him from the beginning, obviously, and when I think of him, there's never been anything other than winning. But you know that. That's why you're all here, to pay big bucks to help my father do the thing he's best at, winning. So I'm going to take a few minutes to talk about something more powerful than winning."

Judy reached underneath the lectern where she'd hidden a Judy Garland–style black fedora and a sequin baton. "I'm going to talk about the power of a spotlight!"

The crowd laughed and so did I because they had no idea what was coming.

"My name is Judith Harrison and I aspire to perform professionally one day. The spotlight lures me. It always has, like a moth to a flame. I sing, dance, and twirl in ways that embarrass those who'd rather I sit still." Again, she looked over at her father, whose head was now in his hands. "Those who'd prefer I turn my lights down to make them shine even brighter."

She stepped away from the microphone and began to twirl that baton so skillfully that the crowd began clapping and cheering. She threw it high up into the air, giving herself time to turn twice, lift her fedora and tip it, before catching the baton again. I jumped to my feet and everyone else did, too. Everyone, that is, except Mr. Harrison.

"I know I'm here to introduce my father, Mr. Jim Harrison, future president of the United States, but I couldn't miss the rare chance to"—she paused to do a few tap moves—"also introduce myself."

The audience absolutely roared.

Multiple courses, appetizers to coffee. More speeches, none nearly as fantastic and unique as my friend Judy's. Wine flowing in abundance. Drunk dancing. So much singing and chitchat and selfies until . . .

My turn.

I stood in the same spot where Judy had spoken earlier. I looked over the audience to see familiar face after familiar face. The Speaker of the House and Congress people and actors and developers and some of the most gifted minds on earth, right there in that room. But I was not afraid.

I'd lost one of the loves of my life. My sister. My Virginia.

I'd resisted my urge to utilize words. Counting them like treasures I no longer deserved.

I'd been lifted up by a woman more powerful than anyone in this room, and her name was Harriet Jacobs. They all paled in comparison.

I knew real power and it wasn't in the ability to afford a fifty-thousand-dollar ticket to a fundraiser or a fifteen-thousand-dollar incremental bid on a Tesla. No. It was in the resiliency to bend one's body forward for seven precious years and go on to rise afterward.

I stood at the microphone without fear or anxiety. I stood brave. I stood ready.

"My sister Virginia should be giving this introduction instead of me. She would lift her chin and make you love her. I will have to stand in for her and I will not do her justice, I fear.

"Still, knowing that, I will speak. Never again will I sit in the quiet. Like my mother, I will own myself and only myself. That is my right. It is all of our rights.

"I am here to introduce you to the most inspiring woman walking the earth, but like Judy, I cannot allow the moment to pass without also introducing myself. My name is Ruth Fitz. I am the daughter of an African American history professor father named Jo and a US senator and future vice president of the United States, Velicia. Sister to a dream, Melody. Sister, too, to Virginia.

"Aside from them, and a few true and lovely friends," I said, looking over at Judy and Franny and Frank and Jane and Sunny and Trevor, "my truest love is language. Words. I swim in them for hours and days and years and hopefully forever. I twist them until they pull emotion from the most inflexible places. I do believe now that I can say with the utmost certainty, I am a Scribe of these times."

After the Election

Dearest Reader:

We lost.

I'm glad we did, actually, because I couldn't imagine dealing with Jim Harrison on a daily basis for four years. Or eight! No way.

I know what you're thinking. Why did we lose? We were doing so well. Yeah, we were. But remember when Mr. Harrison said his beloved wife was missing because she "couldn't handle the rigor"? Come on, you knew it then! She'd caught him in bed with not one but two women he'd met somewhere in Memphis. The rest is political scandal history—Mrs. Harrison leaked the evidence, he hung his head in shame, and the other guy won.

The Fitzes moved back to Birmingham, and with Mom's term up, she joined us in the brownstone. We just sort of fell into our old routine. Rooftop gardening, reading, writing, discussing literature and history. Well, my mother is now a regular talking head on the networks, but it's so very us and I'm grateful for it.

We've even started laughing about Virginia and trading memories of her. We told each other we missed her from time to time. We shared that—missing her—and that brought something close to comfort on the inside.

After the campaign fell apart, Jane hired me on as a social media intern for her staff. I can work from the brownstone and send drafts at my leisure. Well, it's never leisure with a strict deadline. It is Jane, after all.

After the DC fundraiser, we went to twelve more cities, and Judy and I have the magnets to prove it.

I never got another scroll from Harriet Jacobs. I waited for months, but nothing. Then, one spring day, I ventured upstairs to our library floor to straighten up the chaos I'd left before the campaign.

Reorganizing disheveled books and magazines and old newspapers, until a small leather pouch fell onto the hardwood. I opened it to find a key.

Virginia had said it for years—the key to the antique wooden desk would turn up one day. She'd told me it was probably in a jewelry box or a Christmas cookie tin. She swore to me it would make its way back. And there it was, hidden in the books.

I inserted the bronze key into the desk and twisted. It popped open easily and rolled up like an accordion revealing an aged copy of *Incidents in the Life of a Slave Girl* and a blank stack of parchment with a pen resting on top.

I opened the book to the title page to find that it was inscribed.

Dearest, Scribe:

When you write a book of your own, Dear, you will find out what the rest of us already know. The long, meandering, impossible journey to write a full-length novel will nearly take down the strongest of warriors. But nothing will make a Scribe feel more naked than another human reading their sacred words. As I say, counterintuitive it is, but alas, writers are complicated.

I must leave you now, My Scribe. You will forever be my first, but not my last, so I must move along to another who has lost her lovely Words.

I love you, Dearest.

I believe in you.
I bow at your feet.
For goodness' sake, though, write your book!

Forever your
Forescribe,
H✗

Author's Note and Acknowledgment

The first paragraph of this book was written on a particularly upsetting day in the pandemic. I sat at my dining room table with two small children in my charge as the world began to spin out of control. Death all around. Illness rampant. Racial unrest everywhere. Anger on anger on anger, and it was too much.

I held my breath and watched. Then I prayed. And in the end, as I do, I wrote.

From that dining room table, I gave Ruth a pen and told her to write the following words:

My hands feel too small to push against a mountain as tall as racism. Today, like yesterday and the day before that, I am a coward.

Quiet. Calm. Unassuming Ruth. I gave her that line after staring at my own hands for too long. I, too, felt like a coward for not knowing what to say. I continued to write Ruth to prove to myself that quiet does not equal insignificant.

Calmness does not imply weakness. And unassuming makes an ass out of the assumer, not the one who is being judged.

Then, thank God, I remembered Harriet Jacobs.

After seven years in an attic crawl space, she wrote forward. While being relentlessly chased by an obsessed enslaver, still, she wrote forward. Putting herself and her family at great risk, she recognized the power of her small hands, refused silence, and wrote forward.

There were other narratives written by enslaved people back then, but her *Incidents in the Life of a Slave Girl* told the story from the perspective of a woman, adding never-before-seen dimensions to plantation life.

This unassuming Black Mother exposed the hidden world of extensive sexual violence in her narrative. A woman not yet possessing her own freedom wrote her truth in the face of unthinkable hostility and terror. A Black Mother in the 1800s, think of it! Harriet Jacobs knew full well the consequences, and still she released *Incidents in the Life of a Slave Girl* to the world.

In *We Are the Scribes*, I gave her to Ruth, but I really gave her to myself.

Harriet Jacobs carried me through. On the worst days, I felt her. I read and reread her masterpiece to enlighten my darkest places. I drew strength from her words. Her life. Her valor. I reexamined my own small hands and, with her as my example, decided to push.

She is my hero. With my whole heart, I hope that is

apparent in this novel. And in my acknowledgments, I can acknowledge only her.

The first and last words of this book were written in a global pandemic. A plague affecting all of us. A collective reimagining of what it meant to be a human being living alongside other human beings in this fragile world. From my tiny slice of Alabama, I watched many of my neighbors buck the idea of humanity's fragility, and instead, choose strength. But sometimes, a fragile thing deserves to be fragile.

A dandelion crushed in a strong hand isn't destroyed, it is multiplied.

Thank you for reading this Feiwel & Friends book. The friends who made *We Are the Scribes* possible are:

Jean Feiwel, Publisher
Liz Szabla, VP, Associate Publisher
Rich Deas, Senior Creative Director
Holly West, Senior Editor
Anna Roberto, Senior Editor
Kat Brzozowski, Senior Editor
Dawn Ryan, Executive Managing Editor
Kim Waymer, Senior Production Manager
Emily Settle, Editor
Foyinsi Adegbonmire, Associate Editor
Rachel Diebel, Associate Editor
Brittany Groves, Assistant Editor
Michelle Gengaro-Kokmen, Designer
Lelia Mander, Production Editor

Follow us on Facebook or visit us online at mackids.com.
Our books are friends for life.

21982320544160